Can't Nobody

JJV

JJV: the Storyteller Presents:

Can't Nobody

This novel is a work of fiction. Any resemblances to real people, living or dead, actual events, establishments, organizations, or locales are intended to give the fiction a sense of reality. Other names, characters, places, and incidents are either products of the author's imagination or are used fictitiously.

ISBN-13: 978-0-9978472-2-2
ISBN-10: 0997847220
LCCN: 2015942974

For information contact:
www.jjvthestoryteller.com

Acknowledgments

I think about when I was a child in church and would hear the elders always start with, "First, I want to give all the honor to God." And I would wonder why they always said the same thing. Now, I understand because He is the source from which *all* blessings flow, so I am going to start out by saying, I need to give a *shout-out* to my Lord and Savior Jesus Christ. He is the reason for this season.

I attended the Essence Festival 20th-Year Anniversary Celebration, and I became inspired by the people and events taking place around me. I have always wanted to write and have started several books but did not complete them. I knew something was stirring up within me, that it would be different this time. As I was walking out of my hotel room to check out of my hotel, God spoke to me and said, "You will do this. Don't worry about anything because I have commissioned that it be done." So, once I came home, I followed His orders.

I initially did not share what I was doing with family or friends, but I met two people who were traveling from California to Oregon and back, Deborah and Patricia, and went into detail about what I wanted to do. They were both so positive and encouraging. However, I could not have done this without support from my family and friends; thank you for being by support system while traveling through this earthly journey. I love you all. However, my inspiration comes from the Almighty. I love You Lord!

Introduction

I don't understand. That looks like me. Where am I? Why is everybody standing over me crying? Mystery is here and is completely losing it.

"Mystery! Mystery! I am right here. Can't you see me?"

Oh no, Aunt Hattie just ran out of the room, all 350 pounds of her, flailing, and yelling, "Oh, Jesus! Oh, Jesus!"

Let me go get Aunt Hattie.

"Aunt Hattie, what's up?" *Dang! She is fast for a big woman!* "Aunt Hattie!"

Maybe Mystery can tell me what's going on. Let me go back to the room.

Mystery, between her tears, asked, "Doctor, do you think she will wake up soon?"

"She still has a lot of swelling around her brain, but we are remaining positive, and I ask that you do, too."

Can't Nobody

Chapter 1

"Tramp, you can't tell me what to do 'cause you ain't my mama," I shouted at the top of my lungs.

Mystery raised her hand to slap me, and Aunt Hattie ran out of the house and grabbed Mystery's hand. I thought, *I wish she would 'cause I've been waiting for a reason to beat her down.*

"Look. I am sick and tired of y'all arguing and fighting all the time. We are all the family we have. We gotta get along!" said Aunt Hattie.

"Aunt Hattie, Mystery just told me that I would never amount to nothing if I keep doing what I'm doing. I'm tired of her always talking down to me. She the one that ain't nothing!"

Aunt Hattie, with her last bit of strength and energy, said to me, "Don't worry, Baby Girl, about what nobody says about you. It's what you think about yourself and what you believe you can do that matters."

Mystery was my cousin. She was eleven years older than me. Both of our mothers had died at an early age. Her mother died when she was twelve in a car accident, and mine had died shortly after childbirth from some rare form of cancer. I have never seen a picture of my mother because she did not like to take pictures, but I was told that she was a very beautiful woman who suffered immensely due to a rare and incurable form of cancer that claimed her life. No one ever knew who my daddy was because my birth mom never told anyone.

Aunt Hattie was the only mother I knew. She fed me, clothed me, disciplined me, comforted me, and did all of the things that I thought a mother was supposed to do. But Mystery, at age twenty-eight, thought she knew everything about everything and was always telling me what I should do and should not do. I was tired of hearing her bullshit day in and day out. The bottom line was that she couldn't tell me shit because she was just a broke-down stripper who stripped at a hood joint.

"Now, Porchia, you and Mystery get ready for supper," Aunt Hattie shouted as she waddled back into the house.

"Aunt Hattie, I'm going to Tracy's house for dinner."

Tracy was the only friend of mine that Aunt Hattie liked, so I knew I could use her as an excuse. I was really going to meet my girl Chanti. She had been my best friend since fifth grade. She pretty much always had the house to herself. Chanti's mother was never around. Most of the time, she was with her man, Big John, who ran the hood. The young boys looked up to Big John, and the older ones were scared of him, while people like my Aunt Hattie hated him.

Can't Nobody

When I rolled up on Chanti, she was on the porch, smoking a blunt with her man, Sweezy. "What's up, Swoosh?" shouted Sweezy.

Sweezy called me Swoosh because he said, every time I picked up a ball, he would hear, *swoosh*. Sweezy was four years older than us. He was a high school dropout who flaunted his money, cars, and jewelry around the hood. Sweezy worked for Big John.

Chanti had been dating Sweezy since our freshman year of high school. Sweezy was a big guy who sort of favored the late Biggie Smalls, but Chanti liked Sweezy because, besides buying her a car, he gave her money to do the things she enjoyed doing, like shopping and getting her hair and her nails done. We bonded because we both enjoyed fashion and the latest designer releases. Thanks to Sweezy, Chanti dressed the part, while I just looked at magazines. Chanti was one of the most popular and prettiest girls at Booker T. Washington High School. She was hated by the girls and chased by the boys. Although I was told I was attractive, most of the guys looked at me as one of their *partnas*. I loved sports and was the captain of the basketball team.

Mystery was arguing with me earlier because I wanted to go to basketball camp during the winter break, and she was telling me that we could not afford basketball and that I needed to pay more attention to math and reading. She had no idea that I was already taking calculus as an eleventh grader. She probably did not even know how to spell calculus. I noticed that I always had to dumb myself down to deal with most of the people around me. But it was okay, because I enjoyed having these dual personalities. Aunt Hattie always told me that I needed to stop seeking approval from everyone because "can't nobody do me like Jesus." But Jesus did not come with me to school, practice, or down my street when the block turned into a war zone.

"Hey, P! What you getting into, girl?" asked Chanti.

"Nothing, just trying to get away from my psychotic cousin."

"Yo' fine-azz, psychotic cousin," Sweezy muttered under his breath.

"Don't get cut up, Sweezy!" Chanti, half-joking and half-serious, shouted out to Sweezy.

Chanti was known to go off on dudes in a minute. She had put her last boyfriend in the hospital after she found out he was cheating with this cheerleader that Chanti had despised since third grade.

"Boo, you know you are the only one for me," Sweezy said while winking at me.

"Y'all both full of shit," I said, smiling. "What are you two getting into?" I asked.

"We were thinking about going bowling. You wanna come?" asked Chanti.

"No, girl. I'm going to pass and let y'all do y'all's couple thang."

"Ah! Come on, Swoosh. You'll have fun. My boy will join us if you come."

Can't Nobody

One thing that I knew was that I would not be interested in one of Sweezy's boyz. I wanted a way out of the hood, but it was not going to be through selling my body or dating a drug dealer.

"I'm gonna pass. A'ight? I'm out!"

I really did not know what I was going to do. I knew that I did not want to go back to the house, and I also did not want to go to Tracy's. Tracy was a year younger than me, but she was the eldest child in her family. She had four younger brothers and sisters that she took care of because her mother worked two jobs. Her father, who was the pastor of the church that my Aunt Hattie attended, spent most of his time doing "God's business," according to Aunt Hattie. Pastor Charles was a well-known and deeply respected member of our community. And his wife, Tracy's mom, Ms. Carletta, came from a family that had money. They owned five large grocery stores, two cleaners, and the biggest hair salon in town. After Ms. Carletta married Pastor Charles, her family disowned her. Pastor Charles was a former pimp and drug dealer, who had served ten years in prison, but, upon release, he was a reformed man.

Pastor Charles met Ms. Carletta when he was a deacon at the church they belonged to. The story goes that they eloped when she was eighteen and he was thirty-eight years old. Ms. Carletta has not spoken to anyone in her family since Tracy was about three years old. To this day, Pastor Charles has never held a job, but he lives in a large house, gets a new Cadillac every other year, dines at some of the finest restaurants, and takes vacations to Europe.

"Hello."

"Hey, Trace. What you doing? I was thinking of stopping by."

"This would not be a good time, Porchia. I'll call you back!"

"What's wrong, Tracy?"

Silence.

Tracy hung up the phone as quickly as she answered it. I wondered what was going on with her. *Damn!* I thought, *Now I don't know what I'm going to do because I don't feel like having to face that tramp Mystery. I wish it was just me and Aunt Hattie. Life would be so much easier.*

After Tracy hung up, I decided to go to the park to shoot some hoops. I was not dressed to play ball but had some sneakers on. I didn't care; this would allow me to pass time.

"Hey, Shorty! Where you headed?" shouted Poo Man.

Poo Man had had a crush on me since we were in grade school. He was the kid that everyone teased. At twenty, Poo Man was about 4 foot 11 and weighed about one hundred pounds soaking wet. It was odd for him to call me Shorty when I was 5 foot 11. But Poo Man was one of my favorites because he always remained the same. Despite anything that came his way, he was always happy.

"'Sup, Poo Man? I'm on my way to the park. You wanna come?"

"Yo, yo, Shorty! I'll join you." Poo Man quickly darted across the street with a big old grin on his face. Once he got to my side, I grabbed him, picked him up, and squeezed him tightly, giving him a big bear hug. "Okay, Shorty! You're choking me!"

"Ah, I just missed you, Poo Boo."

"Now, don't you go disrespecting me, Shorty. My name ain't Poo Boo."

"Yo' name ain't Poo Man either!"

"Tru dat. Tru dat," Poo Man said, smiling from ear-to-ear.

We walked over to the park, and Poo Man was just talking, but I was not certain what he was talking about because my eye was on the tall guy on the court. I knew everyone in the Ward, but I did not recognize this guy. He was about 6 foot 7 with a creamy dark chocolate complexion, protruding biceps, a six-pack, and an ass that made me wanna slap my mama, *whoever* she was. Just as I was lost in la-la land, he dunked on one of the best guys on the court, and everyone high-fived each other. He stood there with this boyish grin that made me wanna slobber him down from head-to-toe.

Poo Man snapped his fingers and asked me whether I'd heard anything he'd said.

"Who is that?" I asked.

"Oh, I see, you got your eyes on my li'l cousin Ty."

"Yo' cousin?"

"Yeah, that's what's up," said Poo Man.

At that time, the guys were ending their game. One of the guys, Derek, who had a crush on me, spotted me and asked me if I had next. I nodded and noticed that Ty had an almost disgusted look on his face.

"Oh, you think you can hang with us?" asked Ty.

"No doubt. Don't worry. You'll soon find out," I responded.

After I pulled my hair up with a scrunchie, I stepped out and threw the ball to Derek, and I could see Ty had a surprised look on his face. As I drove down the middle and to the basket, a teammate spotted me, and I scored the first two points of the game within thirty seconds of its start. Our team went on to beat Ty's team. I contributed ten points.

After the game, I was celebrating with the guys when Ty approached me and asked, "So, Ms. Lady, where did you learn how to ball like that?"

"Your cousin Poo Man."

He laughed loudly. "Oh, I see you also a comedian."

"You ain't met the other twelve sides of me yet."

"Well, it would be my pleasure, Ms. Pocahontas."

"Oh, I am sorry, we have not been officially introduced outside of me slapping the ball out of your hand. My name is Porchia, and you are?"

"Pleased to meet you," Ty responded with a devilish grin.

"Oh, I see you have no name, so I will call you Sourpuss."

"Ha! You know that you are just too cute, so when will I see you again?"

I began melting, and I felt some warmth oozing between my legs, but I could not let on to him that he was turning me on.

"When you learn how to play ball, Sourpuss."

I shouted "lata" to Poo Man as I walked away, daydreaming about Ty. I was almost home when this car nearly ran me over. I only noticed it because the driver blew the horn at me while swerving to the right to avoid hitting me. That definitely woke me up. Why was I even thinking about this? I did not let anything distract me from basketball or my studies, yet I'd just almost ended my life.

"Okay, I'm glad I woke up. This is bullshit," I told myself.

I looked at my phone to see what time it was. I was hoping that Mystery would have already left for work because I did not want to even see her face. It was 7:00 p.m., so that meant that she probably had left for work. She was pretty diligent about making certain she showed up to the strip club early so that she could cozy up to the club's manager. That way, she could get whatever she needed for the night.

"Hi, Aunt Hattie."

"Baby Girl, we need to talk."

"But, Aunt Hattie, I just got through playing basketball, and I was hoping to take a shower."

That was another reason I'd hoped that Mystery was gone. We all shared one bathroom, and, at times, it was really difficult because Mystery took forever to get ready. She applied makeup like she was preparing for a Lady Gaga contest.

"Baby, I think that can wait," said Aunt Hattie. "I need for you and Mystery to try to work out your problems. All you two do is argue."

"Why are you talking to me about it, Aunt Hattie? She's always starting thangs."

"Baby Girl, sometimes, you must just turn the other cheek."

I know I must have rolled my eyes at Aunt Hattie, but I got tired of her and all of those references to the Good Book.

"Missy, I know you are not disrespecting me."

"I'm sorry, Aunt Hattie, but it is really difficult to get along with her. She always seems to have a chip on her shoulder and be hell-bent on telling me what to do, when all she does is strip at a club."

"Watch your mouth, girl! She's a dancer, and she's trying to help us. She puts food on the table, helps with the rent, and also helps with your school activities. You need to give her just a little break. We are all that we have."

"Okay, Aunt Hattie, I'll try. Can I go take a shower now?"

Aunt Hattie reached over, kissed me on my forehead, laughed, and said, "Go on out of here, Baby Girl. You smell like a pot of spoiled greens."

"I told you I needed to take a shower."

"Hope the soap don't run away." Aunt Hattie always had a way of making me smile, even when I was sad or angry.

"Okay, Aunt Hattie, I'm about to run up your water bill!"

I went to my room to undress and find some comfortable clothes for the house. I was worried about Tracy and, perhaps, would call her after I took my shower. I was caught up thinking about what could possibly be wrong with her when my phone rang. I looked at the caller ID, and it said Unknown Caller.

"Hey, Pocahontas! What's up?"

"How did you get my number?"

"I usually get what I want," Ty responded.

"Well, I guess you did not want to win that game," I smirked.

"Ha! No, Pocahontas. I don't like to beat up on ladies, unless they are into that kind of thing."

"Look, Sourpuss, if you lookin' to hit it and quit it, I ain't the one. I don't have time for bullshit."

"No, just looking for a one-on-one rematch. 'Cause the way you're talking, you want me to beat you."

"Anytime, anyplace," I responded.

"So what about tomorrow after church?" asked Ty.

"I don't do the church thing, but, if you do, we can meet after church at the park around three o'clock."

"Oh, so you're a sinner woman?"

"Only time will tell," I said, grinning, as I hung up the phone.

I immediately called Poo Man to find out what the deal was with his cousin and why he had given my number to Ty.

"Yo! Speak."

"Poo, why did you give your cousin my number?"

"I didn't, Shorty!"

"Well, how did he get my number?"

"I don't know, but it was not me," Poo Man said.

"Why is he calling me?"

"You gonna have to talk to him about that."

"Does he have a girl?" I asked.

"Look, Shorty, you gonna have to discuss that with him."

"Ah, Poo Man! I thought we were homies."

"We are, but I don't get into nobody's business. I told him the same thing when he asked about you."

"Oh, he asked about me?"

"See, there you go. Yeah, and I told him the same thing. I told him, 'You need to talk to her.' Damn! Y'all acting like I'm Chuck Woolery or somethin'!"

"Who?" I asked.

"Never mind, Shorty. But, if you are interested in Ty, you need to get with him. Not me."

"Thanks. You have been absolutely no help."

"Sorry, Shorty."

"Okay, I'll holla at you lata, Poo Man."

"Out," he said.

Chapter 2

I couldn't sleep last night. I was thinking about Ty. I had made it to the eleventh grade without really even having a crush on a guy. No guy had ever gotten to first base with me. Why now?

"Porchia, why is your underwear hanging in the shower? Girl, can you get your shit out of the bathroom? You're not the only one that has to use this bathroom!" shouted Mystery.

"Look, Mystery, I can't deal with your issues today."

I just don't understand why she wakes up with a big chip on her shoulder every day. She was standing in the bathroom door, so I shoved past her, bumping her a little harder than I had intended. She went flying toward the bathtub, pulling down the shower curtain and my things with her. She started fighting the shower curtain, and all I could do was laugh.

Aunt Hattie ran in to see what all of the commotion was about and yelled, "What in Jesus' name is happening here?"

By that time, Mystery was cussing and flailing her arms. I grabbed my things from her and went into my room.

"That girl needs Jesus in her life," I heard Mystery scream. "Aunt Hattie, she just attacked me!"

I could not hear what Aunt Hattie was saying, but I knew that she was playing her normal referee role as she had done on numerous occasions when Mystery and I fought.

It was 8:12 a.m., and I couldn't wait for church to end, so I could see Ty. Aunt Hattie came into my room, saying that we had to talk.

"Look, Aunt Hattie, it was an accident. I was going to get my clothes out of the bathroom as she had requested."

"You two are always going at it for one reason or another. I am getting too old for this, Baby Girl. I need your help. You two have to get along. And you two are too old to fight day in and day out."

Aunt Hattie grabbed her chest and stopped talking. She had a very distressed look on her face.

"Aunt Hattie, what's wrong?" She would not answer. "Aunt Hattie! Mystery! Help! Something is wrong with Aunt Hattie. Call 911!" Mystery ran into the room as Aunt Hattie fell to the floor. "I said call 911!"

As Mystery ran for the phone, I ran to Aunt Hattie. "Aunt Hattie, please stay with us." I could see that she was still breathing, but her eyes were rolling back into her head. "Hurry, Mystery!" I could hear Mystery on the phone with the 911 operator because she was responding to questions. "Mystery, we need an ambulance right now!"

I was trying to get Aunt Hattie up but could not move her. Then, I remembered that I probably should not move her without knowing what was going on with her.

Aunt Hattie was trying to talk, and, at that moment, I could hear the paramedics on the street. Once they got to our house, they rushed in and began working on her. They were trying to talk to her. They immediately took her blood pressure and listened to her heart. They asked me what happened, and I told them that she just grabbed her chest and fell to the floor.

"We gotta move her now," said the young Latina EMT.

After they'd put Aunt Hattie on the gurney, they wheeled her to the ambulance.

"Where are you taking her?" asked Mystery.

"We're taking her to General," answered the Latina EMT.

"Can I ride with you?" I asked.

"No, we'll have to work on saving her life as we transport her," said the short white EMT.

Next thing I knew, the sirens were blasting, and they were hauling off Aunt Hattie.

"See, Aunt Hattie always said we would be the death of her. And, Porchia, this is all your fault," Mystery said through her tears.

"How are you going to blame me when you were the one shouting?"

"C'mon, girl. We need to get to General," shouted Mystery.

I was in my pjs and couldn't go out of the house looking like that.

"Okay, give me a sec to slip on some jeans."

"We may not have a second. Aunt Hattie needs us now."

I ignored her and ran into my room and slipped on a pair of dirty jeans that were on top of my laundry basket and a sweatshirt. Bad enough that my hair was knotted up on my head, but I was not going in pjs, like everyone else did in the Ward. Mystery was looking all over the house for her keys. Typical. She was rushing me and couldn't find her keys. Aunt Hattie would always jokingly tell her it was a good thing her head was attached to her body because she would be in bad shape otherwise.

I didn't have the patience to wait for her to find her keys, so I got the key that I had made that she did not know about. I would, sometimes, take her car when she was either sleeping or too busy to notice that her car was gone.

"C'mon. I got a key."

"Porchia, why do you have a key to my car?"

"'Cause I'm a psychic and knew that something like this would happen and you would have no idea where your keys were. Now, stop with the twenty questions, and let's go!"

"I thought sometimes my car would be parked differently!" screamed Mystery.

"Look, Mystery. Let's stop all of the madness and pull together for Aunt Hattie."

Mystery gave me that "I want to just kick your ass" look, then ran out of the house. I locked the door and ran after her.

When we arrived at the emergency room at General, there were people everywhere. It was so chaotic that I could not tell who was in charge.

"Miss, can you help us? My aunt was just rushed here. She was unconscious," I said.

The Filipino lady responded, "Wait in line."

I looked around and did not see a line, just folks sprawled out everywhere. Some of them were on gurneys in the check-in area. Before I knew it, I had grabbed the hospital worker and shook her, telling her that she needed to help us now. She was totally startled and started screaming. The next thing I knew, security had surrounded us and was pulling me off her. Mystery was standing there with her mouth wide open as security pulled me toward the door. I was flailing my arms, screaming at them, telling them my aunt could be dead, and I just wanted to know what was going on.

After we reached the door, the black guy told the Latino guy that he would handle it. Mystery came running out of the door.

The security guard looked at Mystery and said, "Hey, Luscious."

"What's up, Daddy?" responded Mystery.

"Mystery, we don't got time for no damn reunion! Aunt Hattie needs us!" I said.

Mystery snuggled up to the security guard and whispered something in his ear.

"I'll go and find out information for you and be right back. You wait right here and keep that crazy girl with you," said the rent-a-cop.

"I will be right here, Daddy," responded Mystery.

"Mystery, everything ain't about ho'in'!"

"I'm just using what I have to get information, girl. Now, you need to calm down!" she said.

"I can't. I need to know that Aunt Hattie is okay. And we can't help her from here."

"We can't help her at all. It's up to the doctors to help her," she said.

We went on arguing until the security guard returned and said, "Ladies, we do not have anyone under the name Hattie Mae Williams registered here."

I snapped, "The EMTs said they were taking her here! How do you know?"

"I checked all of the registration, and there is no one by that name," responded Rent-a-Cop.

"If she was unconscious, how could she even tell you her name?" I asked.

"There are no Jane Does here either."

Right when I was about to respond, my phone rang. I could see it was a blocked number. I thought it probably was Ty. I answered hastily, "Hello."

"Hey, Pocahontas! Are you standing me up?"

"I'm at General, trying to find my aunt! She passed out at the house, but they are saying she's not here."

"Okay, let me call you right back," said Ty.

Mystery and Rent-a-Cop had walked away and were talking. The phone rang again with a number I did not recognize.

"May I speak with Porchia?"

"This is she."

"Hi, Porchia. This is Pastor Charles, and I'm at Memorial with your aunt Hattie. The hospital asked me to call you to let you know that she was here."

"Thank you, Pastor Charles. Mystery and I are on our way."

"Mystery, I found Aunt Hattie. We gotta go now!"

As Mystery and I were walking to the car, a guy pulled up in a new black two-door Mercedes convertible. As he rolled down his tinted windows, I saw it was Ty.

"Where you headed to, Pocahontas?"

"My aunt is at Memorial, and we're headed there."

"Are you driving?" asked Ty.

"Yes, I am."

"No, you're not. You look too upset. Come on. I'll drive you," he said.

Mystery put her hands on her hips and shook her head, saying, "No, we ain't riding with no stranger."

"Mystery, this is Ty. Ty, this is Mystery. Now, y'all ain't strangers. Come on."

I pulled Mystery by the hand and opened Ty's door.

"I am not comfortable with this. He looks like a drug dealer," said Mystery.

"Like you have never been with drug dealers before. Get in the car, Mystery!"

Mystery reluctantly got in the backseat.

Ty looked at Mystery and said, "I know Pocahontas can be rude at times, so I apologize for her inadequate introduction. My name is Ty, and I am here to help you."

Mystery asked Ty why he called me Pocahontas.

"Look at her beautiful skin, her silky, long black hair, her tantalizing eyes, and her captivating high cheekbones. She reminds me a lot of a black Pocahontas."

I immediately began blushing at his description.

Then, Ty went on to say, "As a matter of fact, you two look a lot alike with the exception of the hair."

I looked at Ty and rolled my eyes.

"Well, you certainly are a charmer," responded Mystery.

"Ty, can we get this car rolling?" I screamed. "Aunt Hattie is at the hospital, and we have no idea how she's doing!"

"Yes, Pocahontas, I'll get you there in a flash."

Ty pulled off, and I jerked forward. I looked at him, and he was smirking.

"Look! I would like to get there alive!" I said.

"Put on your seat belt, Pocahontas. I assure you that I will get you there safely."

We arrived in what felt like seconds at Memorial. I jumped out of the car before Ty could even stop the car and ran into the hospital. I was running through the door when I ran into Tracy.

"Trace, what are you doing here?"

"My dad called me and told me to come right away. He said that you might need me."

"Where is Aunt Hattie?" I asked.

"She suffered a heart attack, and she's in surgery right now. My dad is up in the family waiting room," responded Tracy.

"Show me where I can find her now," I demanded.

"Porchia, you won't be able to go in. She's in the operating room."

As I was about to plead with Tracy, Mystery and Ty came running in. I had completely forgotten about them.

"Mystery, Aunt Hattie is in surgery," I said between my tears.

Ty grabbed me and began hugging me, telling me that everything will be okay.

"I'll take you all to the family waiting room. The doctor said he would update us on her condition as soon as possible," said Tracy.

She grabbed my hand, and we ran toward the elevator. Ty pulled me and asked me whether I would like him to come.

"Yes, please," I muttered between my tears.

We walked in, and Pastor Charles was sitting there in a stupor. When he saw us, he got up and said, "Daughters, don't worry. Sister Hattie is a strong, praying woman. She will come out of it okay."

I snapped, "How do you know this, Pastor? I did not know that you were a doctor! And why is this happening to such a strong, faithful, praying woman?"

"Daughter, God makes no mistakes. There is a reason for all that happens, and, remember, all things work for the good of those who believe," he said calmly.

"Why should I believe that when your God takes good women away and so many bad people live a long life?" I screamed.

Ty got up and shook Pastor Charles's hand. "Hi, Pastor Charles. Porchia is a little upset. Thank you for being here. I'm sure she appreciates your prayers."

Ty grabbed my hand and said, "Come on, Porchia. Let's go get some fresh air."

"I don't want no fresh air!"

He just grabbed me and pulled me out of the waiting room. Tracy came running behind us.

Once we reached the lobby, Tracy asked if she could speak to me privately. I looked at Ty, and he gave me a wink. Tracy and I walked outside, and once we were out of Ty's earshot, she eagerly asked, "Girl, who is that *fine* piece of chocolate?"

I looked at her and just began laughing sarcastically.

"Aunt Hattie is on her deathbed, and you are inquiring about who I am with. Are you *serious*?"

"I'm not used to you being with anyone, and it looks like he is pretty comfortable with you!"

"Girl, that ain't nobody but Poo Man's cousin. We were supposed to go play basketball before Aunt Hattie had her heart attack. He just happened to be in the right place at the right time."

"Well, seems like he's pretty interested in you, Ms. Hard-to-Get!"

"Trace, stop trying to play matchmaker. I'm worried about Aunt Hattie, and that's my only concern right now!"

"Well, you would be a fool to let that one go."

"How can you tell? You know nothing about him but that he looks good to you."

"What I do know is that you need to stop playing so hard and give him a chance," Tracy said.

"A chance for what? To hurt me like all men are good at doing?" I said.

Ty, then, walked up and started massaging my shoulders and asked, "Ladies, I don't want to interrupt, but I wanted to know if either of you are hungry. I heard that the cafeteria here has some good food."

We both told him no, and I told him I was ready to go back upstairs.

When we walked into the waiting room, Mystery was pacing back and forth. I sat there for a minute until I could not stand it anymore. I shouted, "Mystery, sit your trifling ass down!"

"I can't sit. I'm worried about Aunt Hattie."

"I am, too, but you don't see me walking around like a crazy woman!"

Just as we were about to engage in a full-fledged argument, the doctor walked in with a very sour look on his face. Mystery immediately screamed, "Oh no! We lost her. Aunt Hattie! Aunt Hattie!"

The caramel-complexioned, tall, muscular, and handsome man walked in, looked at Mystery, and said, "No, your aunt will recover. However, it was a very difficult operation. We performed a quadruple bypass. You aunt is lucky she arrived at the time she did."

"When can we see her?" I asked.

"She'll need some time to come out from under the anesthesia. It should take about another three hours or so," responded the handsome doctor.

I looked at his name tag on his uniform, and it said Dr. Little. I thought, *How ironic! Because he is anything but little.*

"I'll keep you updated," he said.

"Thank you for the update, Doc. We'll be waiting here," responded Ty.

Pastor Charles asked us all to gather for a moment of prayer. I rolled my eyes, and Ty grabbed my hand and told Pastor Charles that we would appreciate it. We all gathered in a circle while holding hands. Pastor Charles rambled on and on for about ten minutes. My knees began wobbling, and all I could think about was how I wished he would stop rambling.

Chapter 3

Before Pastor Charles left to go and visit some other patients in the hospital, he told us that he would check back with us. It seemed like we were waiting for days until Dr. Too Fine showed back up to tell us that Aunt Hattie was awake. He told us that she could not take a lot of visitors at one time, and that we should keep our contact short because she needed her rest. I was the first to say that I was going in, and Mystery said she was also. Dr. Too Fine said, "Please, just two at a time, and limit it to ten minutes because your aunt really needs to rest."

Tracy walked over, hugged me, and said, "Tell Aunt Hattie I am praying for her and will come and visit tomorrow."

"Thanks for being here, Trace. I love you."

"Love you, too," she responded.

Before walking out the door, Tracy whispered into my ear, "Treat Ty well."

"Porchia, I would like to hang around, if you don't mind," said Ty.

"You can if you want, but I'm going to try to spend as much time with Aunt Hattie as I can."

I ran out the door in search of Aunt Hattie's room. When I finally found her, she was sitting up, singing,

Can't Nobody

"*Can't nobody do me like Jesus. Can't nobody do me like the Lord. Can't nobody do me like Jesus. He's my friend.*"

"Aunt Hattie, what are you doing up singing?" I asked.

"Baby Girl, I am praising the Lord because I am alive and well. He continues to show favor on all of us, and, if you all don't thank Him, I will."

"But, Aunt Hattie, the doctor said you went through a serious surgery and you need your rest."

"Baby Girl, I will get plenty of rest when I am gone from here."

After helping Aunt Hattie lie back down in her bed, I said, "Okay, Aunt Hattie, that time for plenty of rest might come sooner than you would like, if you don't slow it down a little."

Mystery walked in as I was settling Aunt Hattie into her bed.

"Hi, Aunt Hattie, how are you feeling?" she asked.

"I am so blessed, daughter. Now, come over here and give your old aunt a hug."

Mystery walked over and hugged Aunt Hattie.

"Now, while I have your attention, I need to talk to you two. Look. We are the only family we have. We have to love, care, protect, and nurture each other. All this fighting that you two are doing needs to stop right now. If something happens to me, you two only have each other. So it's time for you to put all of your pride aside and learn how to support and love each other."

Mystery gripped Aunt Hattie's hand and said, "We'll work on it, Aunt Hattie. We just need for you to get better. You are the glue that holds this family together, and we can't do it without you."

Aunt Hattie responded, "I'm getting older, and you two will have to learn how to be each other's glue."

I looked up, and Mystery had tears flowing from her eyes. I thought, *Why is she faking it? She could care less about anybody but herself!* I knew that before I started saying things that might upset Aunt Hattie I should excuse myself from the room.

"Aunt Hattie, I'll give you and Mystery some time to talk. I'll be right back, okay?"

"Go ahead, Baby Girl. They won't let me go anywhere."

I was going to look for Ty and tell him to go home because I did not plan on leaving the hospital. When I walked into the waiting room, Ty was on the phone, and I heard him say, "I need another week because of a family emergency."

When he saw me, he told the person on the other line he would call back to finish their conversation.

"Ty, what family emergency do you have?" I asked.

"You are my family emergency."

"I don't know what that was about, but please do not put off anything because of me."

"I'm just trying to buy a couple more days off work. Please indulge me, Pocahontas."

"I don't want you staying because of me. If you need to take care of business, do it."

"I'm a grown man, and I do take care of my business. And, right now, my business is you."

I started melting again. Feeling that ooziness between my legs. This time, it was coupled with fluttering in my heart. I actually did not like this feeling because it made me feel out of control. The only thing I'd known how to do most of my life was to be in control.

Ty walked over and put his nice, large arms around my waist, pulled me close to him, and softly whispered in my ear, "You don't have to go through this alone."

At seventeen years old, I'd never been this close to a guy ever in my life. I did not know whether to scream and run or embrace and enjoy. So I pulled away and asked him how old he was. He looked shocked by my question and responded that he had just turned nineteen.

"How are you driving a brand-new drop-top Mercedes at nineteen?"

"Where is this coming from? I'm here to show support for you and your family, and you are asking about my car?"

"Look, I have a future ahead of me, and I can't deal with no drug dealer."

"Ha!" Ty said, smiling devilishly. "You and your cousin seriously think that I am a drug dealer?"

"Are you?"

"No, Pocahontas. I am not. If you'll let me take you out to dinner, I'll tell you all about myself."

"I need to go make certain Mystery is not stressing out Aunt Hattie," I said before rushing out the door of the waiting room.

Can't Nobody

I was relieved to get away from Ty because I was very confused and needed to sort out how I was feeling. Before Aunt Hattie's incident, I was all excited to go out with him. But now that this had happened, it seemed like things were moving just too fast. Why did he want to be there for me when he really didn't know me? Why did I want him to be there for me when I didn't really know him? Why was I having these unexplained physical reactions to his presence? This was all just too much to handle and process. I needed to put all of my energy toward Aunt Hattie and not deal with this man that I barely know.

I went back into the room, and Dr. Fine was talking with both Mystery and Aunt Hattie. "Did I miss anything important?" I asked.

"Yes, Baby Girl, I have just shocked the good, young doctor," said Aunt Hattie. "He has never seen such a recovery, but I am trying to tell him that, although he may be good at what he does, God is the ultimate doctor and has the ultimate say-so."

"Aunt Hattie, I'm certain he also told you that you need to take it easy and get your rest," I interjected.

"You are so right, young lady. She does need to rest because we want to ensure that she continues to have a miraculous recovery," commented Dr. Fine.

Mystery was just standing there, holding on to Aunt Hattie like I had never seen her before.

"Doctor, will I be able to stay with my aunt overnight?" asked Mystery.

"I'm certain I can work out something for you, Ms. DuBois."

"Thank you so much, Doctor," said Mystery flirtatiously.

"Well, I could stay, Mystery, so you can go to work," I said.

"It's more important that you make it to school tomorrow, Porchia. I can handle this," snapped Mystery.

Oooh! She gets on my nerves. She doesn't even know how to take care of anyone! I thought angrily. *I cannot leave Aunt Hattie with her.*

As if Aunt Hattie could read my mind, she said, "Porchia, I would really like for you to attend school tomorrow. If you stay here with me, you will be too tired to do anything in school. You know it's important to me that you graduate and go to college."

"Okay, I'm going to ask both of you to let your aunt rest now," said Dr. Too Fine.

I leaned over to give Aunt Hattie a hug and kiss and told her I would be back after school tomorrow.

When I went back to the waiting room, Ty was gone. My heart dropped to my feet. I was really looking forward to seeing him. I also forgot that I had parked Mystery's car at General. *How am I going to get home?* I wondered. Disappointed, I left the waiting room and went down to the lobby. As I walked out of the door, there was Ty, engaged in a conversation on his phone again. He saw me and held up his index finger, indicating that he wanted me to hold on. I rolled my eyes and probably did a little huffing because he ended his conversation quickly.

"Pocahontas, one day, those eyes will get stuck behind your head. And what are you pouting about?"

"I wanted to stay with Aunt Hattie, but she picked Mystery over me."

"I don't know your aunt Hattie, but I doubt she picked either one of you over the other. If she asked you to go and Mystery to stay, I'm certain she had a good reason."

"She said she wants me to go to school tomorrow," I responded.

"That seems like a good enough reason to me."

I started to roll my eyes at him but caught myself.

"I saw that, Pocahontas. I might need to change your name to Roller," he chuckled.

"I don't have time for your comedy show. I need to go get Mystery's car from General."

"Okay." He grabbed my arm. "Let's go get your cousin's car."

"My legs are fine. I can walk without assistance."

Ty let go of my arm and said, "Whatever you like, my lady."

I blushed at him calling me "his lady," although I knew he was being sarcastic.

While he was driving, there was an uncomfortable silence in the car.

"So what's on your mind?" he asked.

"Just thinking about what it would be like to not have Aunt Hattie. She has been the only mom I have known since birth."

"Where is your mom?"

"Your guess is as good as mine. As far as I know, I was put in a basket and left at Aunt Hattie's doorstep. They told me my mom died from a rare form of cancer right after my birth, but I have never seen a picture of her."

"Well, she had to be a beautiful woman," responded Ty. "So do you know your father?" "They act as if he was an alien because I was told that my mom kept my birth father a secret."

"Well, Pocahontas, I like what I see from you so far. I think you are a beautiful young lady. And I can't wait to get to know more about you."

"Are you coming on to me?"

"Yes. Is it working?" he asked, while laughing.

"No, it is not, Casanova!" I said, rolling my eyes.

Ty changed the subject and asked, "Have you eaten, Pocahontas?"

"No, I have not."

"I don't want to hear any back talk from you or see you roll your eyes; we are going to get you something to eat."

"You have not eaten either?" I asked.

"I grabbed something while you were in the room with your aunt."

"Oh, so now you're sneaking around on me?" I teasingly asked.

"I would never sneak around on you, Pocahontas. What do you feel like eating?"

"A three-piece chicken from Frenchy's sounds good to me."

"Frenchy's? I'm going to have to teach you how to eat better."

"Better than what?"

Ty looked at me long and hard and said, "Okay, this time I'll let this slide, but we won't be doing anymore Frenchy's."

I looked at him and rolled my eyes and responded, "According to you."

After ordering my three-piece with red beans, we sat in the car at Frenchy's, idly chatting, while I demolished my chicken. I talked with Ty about school, Aunt Hattie, and Mystery. After devouring my meal, I told him I was ready to go get Mystery's car.

We pulled up to General, and I could not remember where I'd parked the car. The car was not where I thought I had parked it. We spent thirty minutes driving around, looking for the car. I was getting extremely agitated while Ty was "as cool as a cucumber," as Aunt Hattie would say. After scouring the parking lot, I realized that the car was not there. I panicked because, not only had the car been stolen, but I remembered that I had left the keys in the car. I looked at Ty and screamed, "Oh my God! Someone stole Mystery's car!"

Can't Nobody

Chapter 4

Ty was still trying to calm me down when the police officer arrived.

"What took ya so long?" I snapped as the policeman walked up to me.

"Let me handle this, Porchia," said Ty firmly.

It was the first time I heard him say my name, so I was shocked into silence. The young Latino police officer acted as if he recognized Ty, and they stepped away from my earshot.

Within a few minutes, they came back, and the police officer asked me to give him more information on the color, year, make, model, and license plate of the car. I knew everything but the year of the car. Mystery's car was a red Volvo, which she treasured as if it was a new Maserati. Everyone knew it was her car, not because it was the only red Volvo in our hood, but her license plate read "MYST2U."

The rumor was that she'd received the brand-spanking-new car from a married man who she blackmailed when she was seventeen years old. Mystery always told Aunt Hattie that she had saved enough money to buy the car with cash. I guess that was *HER*story, and she stuck to it. The police officer took down all of the information and told me that he would be in contact. He told me that the car should be reported to the insurance company as soon as possible. Immediately, tears began to well up in my eyes.

How am I going to tell Mystery that someone has stolen her car? Ty saw my reaction and quickly thanked the officer.

After he left, he gently grabbed me and said, "It's going to be all right, Pocahontas."

I pushed him back and said, "How can you say that, Ty? Aunt Hattie is in the hospital because of me. Now I let someone steal Mystery's car!"

"It's going to be all right, Pocahontas. All things work out for the good."

"Oh, I guess the next thing that you will tell me is that God will take care of it. Where is this God that everybody talks about? When I need Him, He ain't never around! And if He is such a good god, how would he allow something like this to happen?"

"Pocahontas, bad things happen. Such is life. But God will always be here to support you through the difficult times. But you have to believe in Him."

"Oh, you believe that, huh?" I asked.

"I not only believe it, but I have lived it," Ty responded.

"You know you go around with this hunky-dory attitude, and it's quite irritating. Just take me home!"

The five-minute drive home seemed like hours. I was not certain why I was snapping at him, since he was the only one there for me right now, and we barely knew each other.

"Look, Ty, I'm sorry for yelling at you. I appreciate everything you have done for me today."

"Pocahontas, I want to be here for you, if you'll let me. But it's going to be on you to let me in."

Ty took out a piece of paper and wrote something down and handed it to me. I started feeling the same way I'd felt before when he touched my hand to put the paper in it. I quickly grabbed the paper from his hand and told him thanks. I reluctantly ran to the house when all I really wanted to do was ask him to spend time with me and never leave. The truth was, I did not want to be alone, and he was so comforting. But I could not let this person I barely knew into my life. I kept running until I got to the door and did not look back.

As I walked in, my phone began to vibrate. This was the first time I noticed that I had several missed calls. This time, it was Chanti, and I did not feel like having a conversation with her or anyone else. I had to think about facing Mystery regarding her car. I decided to take a hot bubble bath and think about the best way to break the bad news. While I was preparing my bathwater, the doorbell rang. I was in no mood to deal with anyone, but, when I got to the door, I saw it was the officer that I'd spoken with about Mystery's stolen car.

"Hello, miss, I have some good news and some bad news." I just stared at him blankly.

"We found the car, but the tires were stolen from it," said the officer.

"Is that all the damage?" I asked.

"Yes, ma'am, that's all that we found. The car has been impounded at Joe's Impound and can be picked up by the car's owner tomorrow."

"Thank you, Officer."

Without even thinking, I reached out and hugged him. A little embarrassed from my reaction, I apologized.

"It's quite all right. I understand you've had a long day."

The officer just stood there, and I began to feel a little uncomfortable. He then said, "This might come off as a little odd, but I wanted to see if Mr. Gamble was here, so I could get his autograph."

"Who is Mr. Gamble?"

"The guy that was with you earlier. Tyrese Gamble," he excitedly responded.

"No, Officer, he's not here right now, but I'll let him know that you asked about him."

I watched the officer walk away, and my heart began beating fast. I felt dizzy, as if I was going to pass out. *Am I having a heart attack?* My mind started racing, and I ran to the bathroom for some water and aspirin.

Tyrese Gamble! How did I not recognize that Ty was actually Tyrese Gamble? I knew everything about Tyrese Gamble because he was one of my favorite players. Tyrese played high school ball at Dunbar High School in Beaumont, Texas. Tyrese Gamble was the third player from Beaumont to make the McDonald's All-American Team. Tyrese Gamble was one of the most sought-after players for the NBA after high school, but he determined that he wanted to attend college to pursue a medical degree, and basketball was only a means for allowing that to happen. Tyrese Gamble had a 4.1 GPA after his first year in college. At nineteen years of age, he declared his eligibility for the draft after his first season playing at Miramar State. Tyrese Gamble rocked the sports world when he declared his eligibility. The Birmingham Slammers had the first pick in this year's draft and quickly chose him. Tyrese Gamble was a mixture of Karl Malone and Ray Allen; besides his skills as a power forward, he had a wicked 3-point shot. This officer must have been mistaken! I *knew* Tyrese Gamble.

Tyrese Gamble wore long dreads, was lighter, taller, and bigger than Ty. Ty was chocolate, buffed, and wore a tight fade. How could I not recognize one of my favorite players? I sat around dazed for a while until I decided to go Google information about Tyrese Gamble. After seeing a recent pic of him at an awards show, it was as clear as day that my Ty was Tyrese Gamble. I felt so betrayed! Why would Ty not reveal who he was to me? Why did Poo Man not tell me about his cousin?

I immediately picked up the phone and dialed Poo Man's number.

"Poo Man, I thought we were cool!"

"What's up, Shorty?"

"Why did you not tell me who Ty really is?"

"Ty did not want me to say anything. He was so happy to just be around someone who treated him like a normal person."

"Poo Man, that is fucked up! I would never do that to you."

"Shorty, please do that to me. If you have any rich and famous cousins out there, hook up yo' boy!"

"Bye, Poo Man!"

As I hung up with Poo Man, my phone rang again, and this time it was Mystery.

"Hi, Porchia. Are you okay?"

Why is she all of a sudden being nice? I wondered.

"Yeah, considering Aunt Hattie is on her deathbed, your car was stolen, and my friends are liars, I'm cool!"

"Porchia, did you say my car was stolen?"

"Yeah, but they found it just with no tires, and you can go get it tomorrow morning from Joe's."

"Porchia, what happened? I don't have no money for tires or to pay impound."

"Turn a trick or three. I'm sure you'll get the money."

The minute those words left my mouth, I knew I was out of bounds. The next thing I heard was silence. Mystery had hung up the phone.

I fell on the bed, and tears just began flowing uncontrollably from my eyes. I woke up at 1:16 a.m. with my phone resting on my face and a wet pillow. I looked at my phone and had missed three calls from Tracy, two calls from Chanti, and a text from an unknown number. I assumed it was the impostor. I looked at the text, and it read, "OPEN YOUR HEART AND MIND TO POSSIBILITIES. YOU NEVER KNOW WHERE IT MIGHT LEAD YOU." I knew exactly where it would lead me—to a life full of hurt, lies, and deceit.

I wanted nothing to do with Tyrese or his world! I put on the television and watched a few episodes of *The Housewives of Atlanta* and must have drifted off to sleep because my alarm was going off with Marvin Gaye's "What's Going On?" I smiled as I heard the words because it made me think of Aunt Hattie. She would stand with her hands on her hips and say, while shaking her head, "Baby Girl, you got an old soul listening to that old music all the time."

My thoughts were interrupted when I heard the front door opening. Mystery came in panting as if she had walked twenty miles uphill in the snow.

"Porchia, you are going to be late for school. You need to get a move on."

"You don't even know what time I go to school. Don't come in here acting as if you're my momma!"

"Girl, it would be good if you could just one day wake up happy," said Mystery.

"That is the kettle calling the skillet black. I was doing fine until you came in here with that bullshit," I responded.

"I will not have you disrespecting me anymore!" screamed Mystery.

I just looked at her, rolled my eyes, and walked away before I said something that she would regret.

Can't Nobody

As I walked away from her, everything from yesterday came crashing down on me again. I started feeling the anxiety that I'd felt yesterday after finding out that Ty was not who I thought he was. I did not feel like going to school, but knew I had a test in chemistry that accounted for one-fourth of my grade, and I could not take a chance on not passing chemistry. I thought, *After yesterday, I know that I can only count on one person in this world, and that is me. From now on, I will only concentrate on getting an academic and athletic scholarship to attend the college of my choice.*

Chapter 5

After finishing my chemistry exam, I went to Principal Ashton to ask him if I could be excused for the remainder of the day. I explained what happened to Aunt Hattie, and he actually gave me permission to take the next three days off. He advised me to speak to all of my teachers about my absence. Principal Ashton and I had known each other since I was in the second grade. He was a teacher at my grade school, then my counselor in junior high school. Now, he was the principal at my high school. He knew Aunt Hattie well. They'd both served on Pastor Charles's anniversary committee together for the last ten years.

"Tell Sister Hattie I'll be by to see her soon."

"I will, Mr. Ashton. And thanks."

"Just don't disappoint me. I'm still expecting you to keep up your grades, young lady," he said, smirking.

"That's a deal, Mr. Ashton!"

During the lunch hour, I visited all my teachers to get my assignments for the entire week. The last teacher I visited was Mr. Broomfield, my calculus teacher. He told me we were going to have a pop quiz on Thursday, but he would allow me to take it when I returned. I told him I could take the test now if he had it ready. To my surprise, he handed the test to me and told me that I could go to the back of the room and take it. I glanced at the test, and, for some reason, I lost all reasoning and could not remember basic algebra, much less anything related to calculus. My heart rate increased, and I could feel myself getting dizzy. I was not able to breathe. I was experiencing the same reaction that I'd had when I found out about Ty. I silently talked to myself and tried to reassure myself that everything would be fine.

What I thought to myself must have been really loud because Mr. Broomfield darted to the back of the room and asked me if everything was okay. I could barely make out his features but could see that he had hair missing. After my vision returned, I could see now that Mr. Broomfield had lost his toupee, which I did not know he wore. I told him that I would have to wait to take the test on Friday because I was not feeling well. He told me he knew I would have aced the quiz so not to worry about it. But the real truth was, I wasn't worried about calculus; I was worried about whether I was experiencing the same thing as Aunt Hattie. I was not certain what a heart attack was like, but this was scary. I felt as if I could not breathe, as if I was going to fall out at any minute. I could not fail now because Aunt Hattie needed me.

I rushed home to get some clothes, so I could stay with Aunt Hattie in the hospital. As I was packing my bag, the doorbell rang. I thought it was the Witnesses, so I kept packing, but whoever was at the door would not stop and kept ringing the bell. I already had a very demanding day and was not feeling anything or anyone. Before I got to the door, I saw the Mercedes and knew exactly who it was.

"What do you want?" I hollered through the door.

"Open the door, Pocahontas!"

"My name is Porchia! And I don't have anything to say to you!"

"Pocahontas, listen. I'm sorry for not telling you everything about me, but we have not had a chance to talk. We were both so worried about your aunt."

"It could have started with the introduction at the park."

"What did you want me to say? Hi, my name is Tyrese Gamble, and I am the number one draft pick this year, and I just signed a three-year $20 million-dollar contract with the Slammers?"

"I heard it was $12 million."

"Ha! Don't believe everything you read, Pocahontas. Please open the door, so we can talk."

I reluctantly opened the door, and there he was, holding two-dozen red roses. He was dressed in a white linen short set and was wearing a big smile. His dimples and perfect white teeth were framed by his beautiful chocolate complexion. I wanted to pull the line from *Friday* and say, "Dayuuuum!"

Instead, I managed to keep my composure and asked, "What do you want, Ty?" while rolling my eyes.

"I want you."

"Look, Ty, I don't have time for this nonsense. I'm going to the hospital to stay with Aunt Hattie. She is all I can think about right now."

"I'm not trying to complicate your life, Pocahontas. I just want to share it with you."

"Look, you have a life ahead of you, and all I'm trying to do is graduate from high school."

"And I am not here to change any of that for you. I just want to be here for you. You're special, and I just can't walk away without getting to know all of you."

"Ty, I need to get to Aunt Hattie. I really don't have time for this."

"Okay, Pocahontas. Let me, at least, take you to the hospital."

On the drive to the hospital, Ty was talking, and my mind was running wild. *Why is this guy, who could have anyone he wants, pursuing me? What does he really want? Am I a challenge for him? What did Poo Man say to him? Everyone knows that I'm a virgin, so is this his attempt to take my virginity?* That could possibly happen because I was feeling things for him that I had never felt before, both physically and mentally.

"Pocahontas, what do you think about that?"

"Think about what?" I asked.

He looked at me and asked, "Where are you right now?"

"I didn't hear your question because I'm thinking about Aunt Hattie."

"I asked you whether you would come to Birmingham for a weekend."

46

"What weekend?" I responded.

"I don't know. Some weekend that you feel like getting away from Houston."

"Ty, you are just moving too fast for me. I'm going to be busy with school. I hope to go to winter and then spring basketball camp. I don't have time for anyone or anything in my life."

"I said a *weekend*, Pocahontas, not a lifetime. I'd show you a good time. We're practicing for the season now, but I have some time before we start our preseason to show you around Birmingham."

The whole conversation sounded so unreal to me.

"Give me time, Ty. My priorities right now are Aunt Hattie, school, and basketball."

"You know, Pocahontas, Birmingham is only a ninety-minute flight from Houston."

Ty insisted on coming into the room with me to see Aunt Hattie. When we walked in, Aunt Hattie was talking and laughing with Ms. Carletta. Aunt Hattie stopped dead in her tracks and said, "Oooh, Baby Girl! Who is this fine young man you just done brought to my room?"

Ty showed his beautiful dimples and said, "Well, Aunt Hattie, I see you are doing better. My name is Ty. I am Pocahontas's boyfriend."

"Where you been hiding him, Baby Girl?" asked Aunt Hattie.

Ms. Carletta was looking at Ty as if she was ready to eat him up like a big scoop of Bluebell ice cream on a hot, humid Houston day.

"Aunt Hattie, Ty is just kidding. He is Pooh Man's little cousin," I said.

"Ain't nothing little about him, baby," said Aunt Hattie, chuckling.

At that time, I could have just vanished into thin air. Both of these women were embarrassing me in front of Ty. Ty broke the awkwardness by going to kiss Aunt Hattie on her cheek and telling her it was a pleasure to see her looking so good. He also complimented Ms. Carletta by telling her that the hat she was wearing was stunning. The next thing I knew he was engaged in a full-blown discussion with both Aunt Hattie and Ms. Carletta about fashion. I was so glad to see Dr. Too Fine come through the door.

"Well, Ms. Hattie, what are you doing in here . . . having a party?" asked Dr. Too Fine.

"No, Doctor, these are my partners-in-crime. They are going to help me escape from this place."

"Well, Ms. Hattie, I have good news for you. We'll be releasing you tomorrow, so you can stop planning your escape."

I gave the doctor an astonished look and asked, "Are you sure? Didn't she just go through major surgery? How could you be releasing her so soon?"

Dr. Too Fine looked at Aunt Hattie and asked, "Ms. Hattie, is it all right for me to discuss your medical information with everyone present in the room?"

"Yes, Doctor, they are family."

"As you know, Ms. Hattie had a major blockage of blood from her arteries to her heart. In layman's terms, we performed the surgery to allow an adequate flow of blood to the heart by attaching healthy arteries to the blocked arteries. The normal recuperation time is three to eight days, but, Ms. Hattie, you are our miracle patient. All your vitals are excellent."

"Is there anything that we need to do for her care, Dr. Little?" I asked.

"Yes, Ms. Hattie needs to begin a strict diet. No more greens with fatback, corn bread, and yams. I will have you and Ms. DuBois, along with Ms. Hattie, meet with the dietician about what is okay for your aunt to eat. After Ms. Hattie becomes a little stronger, we'll start an exercise routine."

"Doctor, are you trying to kill me? Exercise?" exclaimed Aunt Hattie.

"No, Ms. Hattie, I'm trying to ensure that you remain with us for a very long time. I'll come back tomorrow for your release, and we'll talk about your follow-up appointment with me."

"Thank you, Doctor. I'm ready to go home to my bed," Aunt Hattie said.

"Oh yes, Ms. Hattie, you have informed the *entire* staff of that," the doctor said, smiling.

Just as Dr. Too Fine was leaving, Mystery entered the room. The doctor stopped and said, "Well, Ms. DuBois, you missed my briefing and the good news."

Mystery responded in her usual flirtatious manner, "Oh, Doctor, do you mind filling me in a little later?"

Dang! She has no shame! I cannot believe she is flirting with Aunt Hattie's doctor in front of all of us, I thought.

"It would be my pleasure, Ms. DuBois. Could you meet me in my office in about thirty minutes?"

Is Dr. Fine flirting back? I wondered.

"It would be my pleasure, Dr. Little," she said with too much emphasis on little.

Luckily, Ms. Carletta ended that odd moment by announcing that she needed to leave to attend a meeting at the church. She hugged Aunt Hattie and went around the room, giving everyone an air kiss on both cheeks.

"That diet and exercise might do you good, too," Ty whispered in my ear.

I whispered back, "You're going to make me cuss your ass out in front of my aunt!"

"Ooh, young lady, I see I will have to wash your mouth out with soap."

"Umm, I see you two are inseparable," Mystery said, smirking.

"Mystery, don't start nothing, and it won't be nothing."

"I guess you two won't be satisfied until you kill me with all that fussing. And mind your manners. Don't you see that we have company?" Auntie Hattie scolded.

"Sorry, Aunt Hattie," said Mystery.

"Aunt Hattie, I hope to be seeing a lot more of you, and, hopefully, you won't consider me as company," responded Ty.

"Well, I'll let you all continue your cozy visit. I think it's about time to go see Dr. Little," said Mystery as she sashayed toward the door.

Ty took the opportunity to take a seat near Aunt Hattie. He turned his charm on and had her eating out of his hand. I hoped that he knew that he was not making any points with me. They were engaged in conversation, and I told them I was going to go use the bathroom as my means of escape. I wanted to go meet with Mystery and Dr. Too Fine, so I could get all of the information that Mystery received. I did not trust that Mystery would understand everything that Dr. Too Fine was saying because she was not exactly the sharpest knife on the block.

I asked the front desk nurse for Dr. Little's office, then I took the elevator up one floor to it. It looked like he had an assistant, but she was not present. I took the liberty to walk to the door that stated "Dr. Little."

I knocked before entering, and, when I walked in, I saw the doctor leaning back in his chair. Mystery was on her knees in front of him. Dr. Too Fine jumped up frantically, trying to pull up his pants, which were at his knees. At that moment, I ran out of his office. *Oh my God! How could she? Mystery tricking herself to the doctor? And how could he have no scruples and allow this to happen?* I ran out of the hospital and ran and ran. I didn't know where I was going but kept running, running, and running.

When I finally stopped running, I noticed that I had run to Hermann Park. I collapsed under a tree and began crying uncontrollably. My life, at seventeen, was spiraling out of control. Aunt Hattie, the rock in my life, was getting older, and the reality hit me that she would not be here forever. This left me with a cousin who was a tramp, who tricked herself to anyone that she thought could help her financially. If that were not enough, I now had this fine, famous, rich basketball player trying to play me for who knows what reason.

God, if you exist, I need some answers. Why is this happening to me? They say that you are a good god, but seems like you like playing jokes with my life. It is not enough that I don't have any parents, but the person you would leave me with, if something happens to Aunt Hattie, is reprehensible. I have tried to be good all of my life. I have volunteered for charity events. I forego my Thanksgiving to work in soup kitchens. I donate both clothes and time to the homeless. I have a good heart and mean no harm to anyone. And this is what I get for all of that?

I shouted while looking up to the sky, "If you think all of this is funny, I ain't laughing!"

Chapter 6

After having a mild meltdown with everybody else's God about my dissatisfaction with my life, the sky opened up, and it began lightning, thundering, and raining super-large drops of rain. I was completely drenched within thirty seconds. I ran to a covered picnic area, soaking wet and crying. In times like this, I could not call anybody but Chanti.

"Chanti, can you come and get me?"

"Girl, Sweezy got mad at me and came and took the car. But where are you? You don't sound good. I can see if Ray could come and get you."

Ray was one of Chanti's "backups" that she would go to when she and Sweezy were arguing. I don't understand why he hung around waiting for Chanti. He was a hardworking guy who would do anything for her, but she did not like him because she said he was square. Any guy who had not been to jail, at least once, was a square to Chanti.

"I'm at Hermann Park."

"Girl. Hermann Park is big. Where at in the park?"

I told Chanti where I was, and about twenty minutes later, she showed up in Ray's car.

"Girl, don't get this car all wet because I may have to give him some of this good-good, if I mess up his car!" Chanti always had a way of making me forget my own problems with her nonsense.

"Girl, shut up. That's who you should be giving your kitty to in the first place."

"You know I don't like Ray like that."

"Yes, I know, because he lives with his parents who have been married for forty years, has no children, don't have gold teeth or wear excessive jewelry, respects women, responds to elders by saying 'ma'am' and 'sir,' and is on the honor roll while working two part-time jobs. Yeah, you bet. I know why you don't like him."

"Girl, there ain't nothing exciting about him. He bores me to death."

"Well, Sweezy gonna be the death of you!"

"Dang, Porchia! Why are you being bitchier than normal?"

I had to laugh. No, she did not just say I was always a bitch. I retorted, "But you love me."

"Yes, I do. A little too much to call Mr. Square to come out to get your butt when it is raining cats and dogs! Where we going?"

"I need to go home. I have had a very difficult day. I need to get some dry clothes. Then, I need to go clean up the house. Aunt Hattie is being released tomorrow."

"Why are you acting so sad? That's great news, right?"

We pulled up to the house, and I was anxious to just get out, so I opened the door before she came to a complete stop.

"I'll get into all that a little later. But thanks for picking me up. I owe you one."

As I was shutting the car door, Chanti yelled, "You owe me waaay more than *one*, girl!"

As I ran up the driveway, I held up two fingers, giving her the peace sign.

The first thing I did after entering the house was run some hot water for a bath. I was still shaking from being in the rain but even more so from what I'd witnessed between the Tramp and Dr. Nymph. He seemed to be a really good doctor. I was not certain how I could ever face him again. Then, I thought, *I need to see if they have another cardiologist at the hospital who could care for Aunt Hattie.*

My thoughts were interrupted when I heard banging on the door. I went to the door and saw that it was Ty, looking like a madman.

"Porchia, I've been looking all over for you. I've called you about twenty times. Where have you been?"

"If it's any of your business, I was out getting fresh air," I said, rolling my eyes and walking away.

"You had Aunt Hattie very worried. Why did you just leave like that?"

"Ask Mystery."

"What are you talking about, Porchia? Mystery said she has not seen you either."

"Yeah, I bet she did."

"Look, Porchia. I'm not certain what is going on between you and your cousin. But, right now, you need to put that aside for the sake of your aunt Hattie's recovery."

"Look, Ty. You don't know me, and I obviously don't know you. So why don't you take your lying ass out of here and let me handle my business?"

Before I knew it, Ty had had picked me up and gently placed me on the sofa. He then kneeled down and put his face very close to mine and said, "Look, you don't have to play this tough-girl role with me. I know that this is hard on you, and I want you to know that you are not alone."

My mind and body went completely limp. I started bawling, and Ty grabbed my head and rested it against his shoulder and stroked it.

In a very calm, soothing voice, he said, "Pocahontas, I am here for you."

****

I woke up startled, and then realized that I was lying on Ty's lap. As I gently attempted to get from underneath his arms, he said, "Hey, Pocahontas, are you trying to leave me?"

I was not certain how to respond to Ty. I wanted him here, and, at the same time, I wished he was not here. He was complicating my life even more. I still had not cleaned the house and prepared it for Aunt Hattie's return home from the hospital.

"What's on your mind, Pocahontas?"

"I have to get this house cleaned before Aunt Hattie comes home."

"You worry about too many little things, Pocahontas."

Ty, then, got up and made a phone call. He returned within minutes and told me he had hired a housekeeping service to come in and clean up the house for me. He also told me he had made arrangements for Aunt Hattie to have a nurse with her from 9:00 a.m. until 6:00 p.m. Monday through Friday for the next two months.

"Ty, how could you make these arrangements without first talking to me?"

"I spoke with the doctor and Mystery, and they thought it was a great idea. You have school, and Mystery works all night and is unable to properly take care of Aunt Hattie without getting the proper rest."

"This is my aunt, and you are out-of-bounds making decisions for me."

"I'm trying to help, Pocahontas. You told me that you needed to concentrate on school, and I'm just making certain you're able to do that."

"You have no responsibility for me. I can take care of myself."

Ty leaned forward, kissed me on the forehead, and said, "Yes, you can, strong lady. I just want to be part of it."

It upset me that I would become such an imbecile every time he did something like kiss me, touch me, hold me, or look at me. He had really become a serious disruption in my life. In order to get him out of my presence, I told him that he was right, and that I was grateful that he was here for me. It worked because he left. I am not a damsel in distress and never would be. I guess Mr. Gamble would have to find that out the hard way!

****

I was awakened by the sound of the doorbell ringing. It was the housekeeper that Ty had ordered. I told her politely that I did not need her service. I hurriedly got up and started cleaning the bathroom, sweeping, dusting, and vacuuming. Before I knew it, I collapsed on my bed, then I heard Mystery telling Aunt Hattie to take it easy. I ran out of the room and saw Aunt Hattie scrambling to get up the stairs. I rushed out to kiss her.

"Baby Girl, what's wrong with you?"

"I'm just happy to see you," I said, while helping her up the stairs.

When she walked in, her eyes opened wide, and she had the biggest smile on her face. "Baby Girl, you have the house smelling and looking like something out of *Better Homes and Gardens*."

I laughed at Aunt Hattie's description and told her I was just happy to have her home. Before she could even get into the house good, the doorbell rang again.

"What is this? Grand Central Station?" I yelled.

"I got it," said Mystery.

I asked Aunt Hattie where she wanted to go, and she said to the kitchen, so I walked with her slowly into the kitchen.

Mystery came back with the biggest and most exotic bouquet of flowers I had ever seen. It had birds of paradise, blazing stars, lilies, and a whole bunch of other flowers I could never name. I knew, by the look of them, they must have come from Ty.

"Well, who in heaven sent me this beautiful bouquet?" asked Aunt Hattie.

"There's a card. Let me read it to you," said Mystery. It says, "THIS IS JUST A SMALL EXPRESSION OF THE APPRECIATION I HAVE FOR YOU, YOUR COURAGE, AND YOUR STRENGTH. HOPE IT ADDS TO THE SUNSHINE THAT YOU ALREADY BRING TO THIS WORLD. WISHING YOU A SPEEDY RECOVERY SO WE CAN GO ON THAT DATE WE SPOKE ABOUT. WITH LOVE, TY."

"He is such a sweet boy, Baby Girl. You need to hold on to him."

"Aunt Hattie, we are just friends."

"If you were smart, you would listen to Aunt Hattie and grab on to him for life."

"I am not looking for anyone to buy me like you are, Mystery."

"All right, ladies, let my homecoming be a peaceful one!"

"Sorry, Aunt Hattie. Yes, you should be resting. I'll go and get your bed together," I said.

"No, Baby Girl, I don't want to go to bed. I have been lying around too long. I would like to go check on my garden."

"Aunt Hattie, Dr. Little said that you should take it easy for the next few days. You should not be tending to no garden," exclaimed Mystery.

"Mystery, I need to do something. I will just curl up and die if I have to just lie around."

I knew that neither Mystery nor I would win this argument, so I went outside with Aunt Hattie.

I was outside watching and listening to her talk about her veggies and when they should be ready when my phone rang. I picked it up without looking at the caller ID.

"Hey, Pocahontas."

"Oh, hello, Ty."

"So I received a call from the housekeeper, and I was told that you refused to let her into the house."

"That is correct. I cleaned the house myself."

"Why?"

"Because I wanted to, Ty."

"Okay, I don't want to argue with you. I just wanted to let you know that I have an emergency that I must attend to in Birmingham. I'm leaving in the next few hours. You know how to get in contact with me if you need me, right?"

"I won't be needing you but thanks."

"Pocahontas, I am not going anywhere, so, one day, you are going to have to let me in."

"Have a safe trip, Ty," I said and hung up the phone. I was glad that he was leaving, and, whether he knew it or not, I did not know how to get in touch with him. I felt some comfort in knowing that he was no longer going to be a complication.

"Baby Girl, are you okay?" asked Aunt Hattie.

"Aunt Hattie, I should be asking you that. Let's go in, and I can make you something to eat."

I thought Aunt Hattie would put up a fight, but she complied and followed me into the house. I realized I did not know what she could eat, so I would have to talk to the Tramp to find out what was good for her.

Aunt Hattie must be some type of psychic because she said, "Baby Girl, I would love to eat some oatmeal, and that is on my list of good things I can eat." Then, Aunt Hattie looked at me, smiled, and said, "You can also add some bacon and eggs to that oatmeal."

"Aunt Hattie, I don't believe that bacon and eggs are on that list."

"Baby Girl, why are you pushing that nice young man away?"

"Aunt Hattie, where did that come from?"

"I heard you talking to him on the phone. Baby Girl, when you find a good man like that, you need to hold on to him. There's nothing wrong with trusting someone. I know it's hard for you, but, Baby Girl, you will not make it through this world without being able to trust. And if you trust in the Lord, you will never go wrong."

"Aunt Hattie, I can't believe that you are ear hustling. But I know what you are going to say next. Can't nobody do me like Jesus," I said, smirking.

"I just pray that, one day, you can develop a personal relationship with Him, so you will have that testimony yourself."

I handed Aunt Hattie her oatmeal and asked her if she wanted anything to drink.

"I want some juice, Baby Girl, but the good doctor told me I could only drink natural juice that is low in sugar."

I began reading all of the labels and realized that I would have to go shopping. I needed to go to the hospital and talk directly to the dietician and, also, find out if I could get another doctor for Aunt Hattie.

"Aunt Hattie, when Mystery comes home, I'll go shopping to make certain you have the right food in here."

"Thank you, Baby Girl, but shouldn't you be in school?"

"No, Aunt Hattie, I have the rest of the week off."

"Now, I don't want you fussing over me. You have a life to live and a young man to catch."

I shrugged my shoulders and told her, "There is just no winning with you." Then I hugged her and went to the room to prepare to do my day's chores.

Chapter 7

As I was walking out the door, Pastor Charles was coming up the walkway.

"How are you doing today, Porchia?"

"I'm fine, just about to do some things for Aunt Hattie."

"Well, it would be nice to see you in church sometimes, young lady."

"Yeah, and it would be nice to see you mind your own business sometimes, Pimp Charles," I muttered under my breath.

For some reason, this man just irritated me. As I kept walking, I heard him say, "God loves you, and so do I."

I had too much to do without him adding craziness to the start of my day. But his presence reminded me that I needed to call Tracy. She had called me several times, and I was yet to return her call.

I was at the bus stop when this guy I recognized from my school stopped and asked me if I needed a ride. I told him that I was good and would just wait on the Metro and that it should be arriving in a few minutes. He then asked me if I knew Chanti. I told him yes, that was my girl. He then went on to tell me that she and Sweezy had been shot. I was not certain what happened after that because I blacked out. When I woke up, I was sitting in his car, and he was asking me if I was okay. I told him I had not eaten for a while but remembered he had said something about Sweezy and Chanti.

I asked frantically, "Did you say that Chanti had been shot?"

"Yes, something about Sweezy messing with one of his rivals' women. The dude rolled up on Sweezy and Chanti at the Stop 'n Go and shot up the car."

"How are they?"

"I don't know, but they were both taken to General."

I screamed, "Can you take me there now?"

"No problem."

When we rolled up to General, Chanti's mom, Cherelle, was outside hollering and crying while Big John was trying to calm her down. I jumped out of the car and ran up to them. Cherelle looked at me and screamed, "She's gone!"

"What are you talking about?" I asked.

Big John looked at me and said, "They killed her."

I felt my legs crumbling right under my body, and I could not stand any longer. I went down to the ground and banged the concrete, screaming, "NO! NO! NO!"

The guy who had brought me to the hospital jumped out of the car to help me up.

When he picked me up, he noticed that one of my hands was bloody. "We need for them to check you out."

"No! I'm good. I want to see Chanti!"

Big John said that was not a good idea because her body was not in good shape.

"Please! Please! I need to see Chanti!" I screamed.

Cherelle gave the hospital permission for me to see Chanti. When I went to the room where she was at, there was a white sheet over her body. I immediately began to feel that this was a bad idea. My heartbeat increased drastically, and I started feeling faint. The hospital attendant asked me whether I was sure I should do this. I told him yes. I *needed* to see her. He pulled back the sheet and half of Chanti's face was missing. I let out a scream that could have awakened the dead. The hospital attendant quickly covered up Chanti's face and escorted me out of the room. I collapsed to the floor, bawling.

"Miss, can I do anything for you? Is there anyone here with you?"

I shook my head and asked him to just leave me alone.

"I can't leave you here, miss."

"Just give me a few minutes!"

While I was sitting in the middle of the floor crying, I heard a familiar voice, "Porchia?"

I looked up, and it was Dr. Nymph.

I wanted to ask him what was he doing at General when he worked at Memorial, but what came out of my mouth was, "Oh no. Not you. Leave me alone and go find someone to suck your dick!"

Dr. Nymph picked me up by my arm and escorted me away from the area. I was so weak that I could not fight him, so I just followed. I felt creepy with him touching me. *That's okay. Dr. Nymph won't be around for long if I have anything to do with it*, I thought.

Dr. Nymph led me to a conference room in the hospital, and, once we sat down, he asked, "Porchia, what's wrong?"

"I should be asking you what's wrong with you—taking advantage of your position as a doctor for sexual favors."

"Porchia, I do apologize that you walked in on me and Mystery, but it's not what you think."

"So, Doctor, what do you think I think?"

"I don't really want to discuss that right now. I'm more concerned about your well-being."

"Well, I was on my way to the hospital to find out the procedures for reporting an ethics violation against a doctor and to see if I can get Aunt Hattie another doctor!"

"Porchia, I understand your concerns, and I want to let you know that nothing like that has ever happened before. I have fallen in love with your cousin."

"Ha! In love? I guess I should call you Dr. Strange Love."

"Porchia, the truth is that meeting your cousin at the hospital is not the first time we met. I have known Mystery for a long time. I go and watch her dance often. I may be guilty of a crime, but it is not the one you think. I have not taken advantage of your aunt's condition to get any special favors. Spending time with

Mystery has allowed me to confess my real feelings for her."

I could not believe what I was hearing. I just stared blankly at him.

"I love Mystery, but she does not feel that she is worthy of my love. I am going to prove to her that she is very worthy." He, then, pulled something out from his pocket. It appeared to be a small jewelry box. "I've been carrying this around with the intent of asking Mystery to marry me but have not found the right time."

I took the box out of his hand and opened it. Inside was the biggest sparkling diamond ring I had ever seen! *Dang! The Tramp must give good head to deserve a diamond like this!* I thought.

"Dr. Little, I would advise you to get to know Mystery before you go messing up your entire life. There is more to life than good sex."

"Porchia, no disrespect, but you are only a child. You still have plenty to learn. Open up your mind and heart. On that note, if you are okay, I will get on with my business."

As I watched Dr. Dumb walk out of the room, I was still in shock. My life was like a cyclone that would not stop. My best friend was dead, and my tramp cousin was getting married to a doctor! Oh, I needed my girl Chanti to just make everything okay. She had a way of making me forget about my troubles. *No, Chanti, you can't leave me now! We did not get the opportunity to talk about Ty. You're the only one that I can talk to about anything and everything. Oh, girl, what have you done? Why have you left me?* I just put my head on the table and cried, cried, and then cried some more. It seemed like I was in there for hours before someone entered the room and asked if he could help me. I told him that I had just finished a conference and was about to leave.

As I left the room, I ran into Big John and asked him what he was still doing there.

"Sweezy has just been moved out of ICU and into a room, so I'm on my way to see him."

"You mean that bastard is still alive?"

Big John looked at me startled. "Yes, he is!"

I shouted, "He's the one that should be dead. No one was after Chanti! She's the innocent one in this! But he is *still* alive while Chanti is dead!"

"Look. I'm sorry about losing Chanti because she was like a daughter to me, but Sweezy is also like a son to me. I don't like you talking that way about my boy. Yes, it's messed up that Chanti got caught up, but she knew the game."

"What the fuck game are you talking about, man?" I screamed.

At that moment, a security guard passed by and asked if everything was okay. I knew, at that time, I needed to get away.

Chapter 8

I did not want to go home. This was the time I would have called Chanti. Sadness engulfed me, and I did not know where to go or who to turn to at this moment. My phone rang, and it said Unknown, but I knew it was him. I answered the phone, trying to sound strong, but he immediately asked me what was wrong.

"My girl Chanti was killed today."

"What? What happened?"

"I really don't know. I was told some guy was after her boyfriend and shot both of them. But she's dead, and he's alive!"

"Okay, I'll be back tomorrow."

"No, you have been away long enough. Your season starts soon, and you need to take care of business."

"You *are* my business, Pocahontas." He paused. I guess he was waiting for me to say something. Then he asked, "Is the nurse working out?"

"I don't know. I haven't been home since early this morning. I'm on my way there now."

"Pocahontas, can you make me a promise?"

"Not without knowing what you want me to promise."

"Could you promise to call me when you need me?"

Feeling very vulnerable at the time, I whispered, "I promise."

"I'm here for you, Pocahontas."

"Yes, Ty. I think you have told me that several times."

"And I will keep on telling you until you start believing it. Well, I need to go, but I'll call you soon."

I was relieved that our conversation was ending because the odd feelings were coming back, so I said, "Bye," and hung up the phone.

As I walked to the bus stop, I wished I could go far, far away from here. I didn't know how much help I could be to Aunt Hattie right now. And I definitely did not want to see that tramp of a cousin. *How stupid could the doctor be to fall for her?* As I was thinking about the situation, the bus pulled up and almost left without me even noticing. I got up and had to run and knock on the door.

"Hi, there. My bad. I didn't know you were waiting on this bus."

"It's all good. I was just preoccupied and didn't see you coming. Thanks for opening the door."

"My pleasure, young lady," said the burly old man who reminded me of a black Santa Claus.

Although the ride from the hospital required me getting on three different buses, I was glad that I had to time to just chill. I decided to take out my phone and listen to some music. I was listening to Tamar Braxton and was fine until she started singing "All the Way Home." It was a combination of the loss I was feeling for Chanti and my feelings for Ty. My emotions were a mixture of anger and fear. I was so mad about Chanti leaving me and afraid that I could not survive without her. *So is this what their god does? I definitively know that I want no part of him!*

When I arrived, a middle-aged Filipino lady was walking out the door. She greeted me by saying, "Hi, you must be Porchia. My name is Leilani, and I'll be caring for your aunt."

I put on a chipper voice and responded, "Nice to meet you, Ms. Leilani. I'm sorry that we did not get to speak earlier. But will you be here tomorrow?"

"Yes, I be here around 8:30 a.m. So I will see you then."

"Sure. Well, good night."

"Good night, Porchia."

I walked in, and the house seemed eerily quiet. I looked into Aunt Hattie's room, and it was pitch-black. I could see that Mystery was not in her room either. I walked to the kitchen and heard Aunt Hattie saying, "You know the Good Lord always looks after His sheep."

The familiar male voice responded, "Yes, He is good all the time."

Aunt Hattie responded, laughing, "All the time He is good."

I could not stand to listen to them talk about this good God, so I escaped to my room.

I flopped down on my bed that I had not made in days and saw a piece of paper. I wondered where it came from. I guess now the Tramp was leaving me notes instead of talking with me after she was found on her knees. I picked it up, and it read: "YOU ARE NOT

ALONE. WHENEVER YOU NEED ME, I WILL BE THERE. I AM JUST A PHONE CALL AWAY. 555-777-9311, TY."

I need him more than I need air right now. I want him to be right next to me, holding me, comforting me. I was tempted to call him but held back because I knew he needed to be right where he was at this time. He was a new player on the team and needed to support his position, although it would be no surprise to anyone that Tyrese Gamble would be the starting forward for the Slammers. Ty not only needed to be there for his coach and the organization, but it was even more important that he be there for his fellow teammates.

"Porchia, honey, are you in there?" screamed Aunt Hattie.

If that woman does not stop screaming she'll have another heart attack, I thought.

"Yes, Aunt Hattie. I'm here."

"Well, Principal Ashton was just leaving and wanted to say bye."

I rolled my eyes because I did not feel like seeing anyone or pretending that I was okay. But I put on my happy face and walked out of the room, smiling. "Hi, Mr. Ashton."

"Well, hello, there, young lady. Just wanted to make certain you were okay. I heard what happened to your friend Chanti."

"Yes, Mr. Ashton, I'm fine."

"Well, I want you to know that you have my condolences."

"Thanks, Mr. Ashton."

"I know you're supposed to be back to school on Friday but just make it a long weekend. You've had a lot on your plate."

"Thanks. Will do."

Little did he or anyone else know that I did not want to go back to school at all and was thinking about taking independent study to complete the school year.

"Okay. Take care, young lady. And if you need anything, please do not hesitate to call me."

"I will, sir."

Principal Ashton kissed Aunt Hattie and also told her that he was always just a phone call away. When Aunt Hattie closed the door, she looked at me with pain in her eyes and said, "Baby Girl, let's have some coffee."

Aunt Hattie and I walked into the kitchen, and I grabbed the coffee from the cabinet and two cups.

"Baby Girl, I'm not completely helpless; I can do this."

"Aunt Hattie, you better take advantage of this now, because soon, you'll be back to serving me."

Aunt Hattie laughed and said, "Baby Girl, if you don't get out of my way so I can make this coffee . . . 'Cause the last time you made coffee it tasted like mud."

"How do you know what mud tastes like, Aunt Hattie?"

"If only you knew," she said while laughing loudly. She continued to prepare the coffee while singing "Jesus Is on the Main Line."

After she poured two cups and sat down, I said, "Aunt Hattie, are you supposed to have coffee?"

"Girl, I don't know but drink up," she said, laughing. "Baby Girl, I know you've had a difficult week."

I thought, *You do not know the half of it.*

She continued, "Me in the hospital, your friend dying."

"Aunt Hattie, Chanti did not die; she was killed!"

"I know, baby, but you have always tried to be strong, even as a young child. Things would happen, and you would go around trying to take care of everybody, but now it's time to take care of yourself."

"I have been, Aunt Hattie."

"No, child, you have not. You are trying to push away a good young man who obviously cares for you. You keep everything all bottled up inside you. That ain't good. You will blow up one day."

"But—"

"Listen, Baby Girl, there is someone who will always be here for you, but you have to let Him in."

"Aunt Hattie, I am not prepared to listen to a 'come to Jesus' speech tonight."

"Porchia, one day, I pray that you will open up your heart to Him. He does not only take care of your needs, but He provides for your wants. When I say 'can't nobody do you like Jesus,' Baby Girl, that comes from the trials and tribulations I've faced during my lifetime. I know you see me as good ol' Aunt Hattie. But there was a time when I was hell on wheels and lost like a needle in a haystack. Chile, God delivered me, and that is why I'm the person I am today. I can't do anything without Him. He is the source from which all of my blessings flow. Why do you think I am out of the hospital right now? It was His healing hands! And believe me, as I am sitting here today, one day, you will know Him for yourself. I know He answers prayers, and He will answer my prayer that you are saved before I depart from this earth."

"Well, Aunt Hattie, I'm glad to hear that you'll be around for a long time."

Aunt Hattie, both disgusted with my response and amused, playfully slapped me on top of my head.

"Okay, don't have me calling Child Protective Services on you."

Aunt Hattie got up from the table and hugged me, saying, "Baby Girl, you will be all right."

After washing out our cups, I walked with Aunt Hattie to her room. She wanted to watch *Dancing with the Stars*, so I lay in bed with her and watched the show. At this time, there was no place I would rather be other than lying in a fetal position next to Aunt Hattie. For some reason, she always made me feel very safe.

Can't Nobody

Chapter 9

I was awakened from a sound sleep by the need to use the bathroom. When I woke up, I realized that I had fallen asleep in Aunt Hattie's bed. Aunt Hattie was nowhere to be found. I ran to the bathroom and, upon exiting, met up with the Tramp. Mystery was standing there with her hands on her hips.

"You are not a baby. You should not be sleeping with Aunt Hattie. Aunt Hattie is trying to recover and needs to rest in peace."

That was a dig because I'd slept with Aunt Hattie until I was about nine years old.

"Go suck a dick!" I went into my room and slammed the door. I just didn't understand why she always had to start things with me. It seemed, the older she got, the more intolerable she became. I needed to get out of there. I was going to head to basketball practice after I spoke with the nurse. I was not certain what I should or should not be doing to help Aunt Hattie.

Something in me told me to go check on Cherelle. I noticed that there was a nice, cool breeze in the air. By the time I reached Chanti's house, my mind was a little bit easier. I saw Cherelle's car sitting in the driveway, so I ran up to the door to knock on it. I noticed it was cracked open.

I yelled, "Cherelle! Cherelle!"

I thought it was odd that Cherelle would leave her house open like that. Maybe she was with Big John at the hospital. I took out my phone to call her, and, when it rang, I heard the phone ringing in the house.

I opened the door to find Cherelle slumped over on the sofa.

"Cherelle! Cherelle!"

I immediately dialed 911, letting the dispatcher know that I'd found Cherelle unconscious. The dispatcher asked me all sorts of questions, and I kept telling her that I did not know. The dispatcher finally told me that the paramedics were on their way. When I hung up the phone, I saw that there was an empty bottle of vodka and a bottle of pills lying near her, on the sofa.

"No, Cherelle! What have you done?"

When the paramedics arrived, they immediately started working on Cherelle, but, shortly after arriving, they pronounced her dead from what looked like a drug overdose. I sat in the chair that I normally sat in when visiting Chanti with my head in my hands. I had no more tears. I could not conjure up enough energy to do anything. I could only imagine what had been going through Cherelle's mind after losing Chanti. Yes, Cherelle had Big John, and Chanti had Sweezy, but, when it came down to it, they really only had each other as family. Cherelle was an only child who only had distant cousins. Chanti had pretty much grown up alone, though she did socialize with many people. She always said that she had many associates but few friends. She loved her mother deeply, even though she'd spent very little time with her. And it was evident that Cherelle did not feel she was worthy of living without her daughter. Or was she filled with guilt for not being there for Chanti? My heart went numb. I no longer knew what to do or think.

"Ma'am, is there anyone we should call?" asked one of the paramedics.

"Yes. But I am not certain how to get in contact with him."

"Well, we're going to take the body to General. Perhaps you can let the next of kin know."

Why are they being so impersonal about my best friend's mother? They're acting as if she's an object instead of a person. I did not have the energy to discuss anything further with them, so I told them I would do so.

I sat in the chair until I could not feel my legs anymore. Finally, I got up and walked into Chanti's room. She had clothes thrown everywhere. Seemed like she had just been shopping because most of them still had tags. I lay down on her bed, closed my eyes, and thought about the days when we would just lie here and talk about boys, school, friends, and frienemies. It seemed as if I could smell Chanti's scent, which made her seem alive to me.

After spending hours in Chanti's room, I went to get Cherelle's phone to see if I could locate Big John.

"Hi, Big John."

"Yeah, who dis, and why are you calling from my woman's phone?"

"Big John, it's Porchia."

"Porchia, why are you calling from Cherelle's phone?"

"Big John, something bad has happened."

"Go on, girl. What?"

"I came over to visit Cherelle, and the door was open."

"Girl, what happened?" Big John asked, sounding impatient.

"Well, I opened the door and found her slumped over on the sofa, so I called 911. Big John, she's dead!"

There was complete silence on the other end of the line.

"Big John, are you there?"

Big John responded calmly, "I'm out," and hung up the phone.

Chapter 10

I just wanted to check out of school, basketball, society, and life, but I found that staying busy actually helped me cope with what was going on. The school provided counseling for those of us who were close to Chanti. I felt it was a joke. How was someone who didn't know me going to help me deal with my grief? *I am supposed to be attending the funeral today*, I thought.

Big John called me back shortly after I called him and told me not to mention anything to anyone about Cherelle killing herself. He asked me to say that I found her slumped over and called 911. That's all. I did not like lying, but I guess I would not be lying, just would not be telling the whole truth. Big John had also cleaned out the house and brought me things that he thought I would appreciate, like pictures of me and Chanti, her poetry, her jewelry box, and her diary. I have not had the strength yet to look at her diary and thought maybe I should not.

****

The funeral would start at 11:00 a.m., and it was now 10:00 a.m.

I said out loud, "Chanti, you know I don't do church, but I am doing this for you, girl."

"Porchia, are you ready?" screamed Mystery.

"Almost," I said.

Can't Nobody

"Me and Aunt Hattie about to walk out the door! C'mon, girl!"

I hurriedly slipped on some slacks and a blouse. My hair was a mess, so I just pulled it up into a bun on the top of my head and added a headband. I went to Chanti's jewelry box and took out her pearls to put over my blouse. I thought about Chanti looking at me, trying to give me a makeover. Although I thought my eye for fashion was equal to hers, she would never let me dress myself for dances. She would clothe me and put on my makeup. *Well, this will just have to do for today,* I thought while looking in the mirror.

We drove up, and the parking lot was filled. We had to park three blocks away from Better Hope Tabernacle. This church was one of the larger black nondenominational churches in Houston. I'd once heard Pimp Charles boasting that he had a membership of 25,000 people. While walking up to the church, a white limousine pulled up. I thought it was Big John and Sweezy. Well, when they got out, I realized it was not Big John and Sweezy, but Poo Man and Ty.

My mouth dropped because I had just spoken with Ty, and he had not mentioned he was coming. I saw Poo Man nudge Ty, and Ty looked our way. I could see his dazzling white teeth and dimples from where I stood. I hoped I was not smiling too much because I certainly felt my heart clapping and doing a happy dance.

"What are you doing here?" I asked as I looked at him.

Can't Nobody

"I came to support my girlfriend while she attends her friend's funeral. What are you doing here?" he said, smiling as he leaned over and kissed me on my cheek. He then went to greet Aunt Hattie and Mystery. He took Aunt Hattie's arm to escort her into the church. I followed behind them with my heart still clapping.

The church was filled, and we were looking for a seat when an usher approached me and said, "We have reserved seats for you with the family up front."

"Are there enough seats for all four of us?"

"Yes, sister, there are."

The usher escorted us to the second pew where Big John and Sweezy were. There were also a couple of other folks there who I did not recognize. Big John acknowledged us, while Sweezy did not even look up. He had sunglasses on and was sort of slumped over in his seat. Ty put out his hand for me to walk, so I had to sit next to Sweezy. Ty took the seat next to me while holding Aunt Hattie's hand, so she could follow him. There was a strong stench of liquor coming from Sweezy. He was stiff and not moving. I reached out and took his hand and held it. This was the first time he even recognized my presence.

He started yelling, "I am sorry! I am so sorry, Swoosh! It's all my fault. I'm sorry, Chanti!"

One of the guys I did not recognize got up and escorted Sweezy out of the sanctuary.

I began crying, and Ty gave me a handkerchief. I lay my head on his broad shoulders. I lifted my head slightly and whispered between my sniffles, "Who in the hell are all these people? They did not have this many friends."

Ty responded by wiping my eyes with his fingers.

We sat through hours of people talking and singing. Then, Pimp Charles got up there and whooped and hollered about who knows what. I had completely checked out by then. I was just glad that both of the caskets were closed. It would have been unbearable to see them lying in a casket next to each other had they been open. Big John had obviously spent a lot of money because the caskets looked like they were made from platinum, and there were flowers everywhere. It reminded me of the many celebrity funerals that had been televised. I was briefly entertained by people crying and falling out, knowing that they were not that close to either of them.

The time finally came where we had to exit the church, and the family was allowed to go first, which included us. When we got outside, Sweezy was standing next to a black limousine. Big John told me that we could ride with them to the cemetery and the repast. I told Big John that although I could not go to the cemetery, I would get with him later. He was so much the opposite of Sweezy. Sweezy looked like a broken man who was trying to do anything he could to take his next breath. Big John looked like he was in control of the world and everything in it.

I walked over to Sweezy, and he was still crying.

"Sweezy, it is not your fault. You did not have control over someone else's actions. You need to forgive yourself."

He just looked at me while still crying.

"Sweezy, I'll talk with you later, okay?"

He hugged me. He smelled like cheap liquor, weed, and cigarettes. I started feeling faint, so I pulled away and told him to be strong.

I walked up and heard Aunt Hattie say, "Although this was a sad occasion, it was a beautiful ceremony. And Pastor Charles brought the Word."

I rolled my eyes. Ty caught me and gave me a stern look. I interrupted the next thing that Aunt Hattie was going to say by asking, "Are we just going to stand here all day?"

"Are we going to the graveyard?" asked Aunt Hattie.

"Aunt Hattie, you all are welcome to go, but I can't do it."

"Well, Baby Girl, if you are not going, I am not going."

"Come on, ladies. I would like to take you all out to eat."

"I'm not hungry, Ty."

Ty looked me up and down and said, "Pocahontas, it looks like you have not eaten in weeks. You're getting a little scrawny."

Aunt Hattie interjected, "I'm hungry and will be glad to accompany you, handsome."

"Well, all right. Is anyone in the mood for some Pappadeaux's?"

Mystery screeched like she had never had food before.

"Well, let's do this, ladies."

The chauffeur got out and opened the door for us. Then we piled into the limousine.

****

When we arrived at Pappadeaux's, there was a line of people and what seemed to be a two-hour wait. I told Ty that we should go somewhere else because the wait would be too long.

"When you are hanging with Tyrese Gamble, there is no wait," he whispered to me.

For sure, we were escorted to a table shortly after we walked in.

Aunt Hattie seemed just as happy as she could be. She did a good job with ordering and stayed away from fried foods. She had grilled fish and vegetables. Mystery, being in her normal fashion, ordered lobster and filet mignon. I ordered the lobster bisque and a seafood salad.

Ty looked at me and said, "You know I like my woman to have a little meat on her bones. Girl, eat up!"

"Well, you better go find her because this is about as much meat as you will get on these bones."

Once all of our food arrived, Ty's order looked the best. He'd ordered a large heaping of everything that was fried. I wondered how he would be able to eat all of that and still go up and down the court.

Can't Nobody

Aunt Hattie, Mystery, and Ty sat around talking, while I was deep in thought about Sweezy. I had never seen him in that condition before, and I was worried. I knew that Chanti loved him, and I did not want him to do anything crazy like Cherelle. I was thinking of a way that we could meet up and have a discussion. I thought about how I initially blamed him for what happened and played out the "but for" logic over and over again in my head. I realized that I needed someone to blame besides the god that everybody talked about. But the bottom line was, he had no control over what happened. He could not take this burden and carry it around.

"Earth to Pocahontas. Earth to Pocahontas."

"What, Ty?"

"Are you ready to go? I've already asked you several times."

"If you are, I am."

The chauffeur drove us back to our house. Aunt Hattie was thanking Ty for coming to Houston and telling him that was her first time riding in a limo. She went on to tell him that she appreciated the way he looked over me. Mystery mumbled a thanks that did not seem sincere. Not certain what that tramp's problem was today, but I was not feeling it or her.

After Aunt Hattie and Mystery went into the house, Ty sat on the porch and grabbed my hand. He guided me, seating me beside him.

"Pocahontas, I'm leaving tomorrow. I would like for us to spend some time alone before I go back."

"Sure. Let me go change clothes, and we can do that."

"Okay. I'll be in the car waiting on you."

I ran in the house and told Aunt Hattie I was going to hang out with Ty.

"Baby Girl, I'm glad you have come to your senses about that boy. One like that does not come around every day."

"Aunt Hattie, you're acting like Mystery right now."

"Baby Girl, it ain't got nothing to do with how much money he has or him driving us around in a limo. That boy has a good heart, and he cares about you a lot!"

"Okay, Aunt Hattie, I need to change clothes."

I had not washed in days but was able to find a clean pair of jeans and a Cowboys sweatshirt. I didn't know what Ty wanted to do, but hopefully, my clothing choice would be okay. I looked at my dresser and saw Chanti's diary. For some odd reason, I grabbed it and put it in my purse as I ran out the door.

"Bye, Aunt Hattie."

Chapter 11

Ty and I hung out at one of his cousin's "hole-in-the-wall" establishments on OST. I probably should not have been drinking but had a couple of margaritas and two shots of tequila. We shot pool, threw darts, and danced. This was the first time I'd had fun in a long time.

"It is getting pretty late, Pocahontas. I probably should be taking you back home."

"The night is still young, Ty. Are you trying to get rid of me?"

"I have a flight in the morning, so I have to get an early start."

"Where are you staying?"

"I'm staying at Hotel ZaZa."

"Where in the hell is Hotel ZaZa?"

"It's not too far from here."

"Can I go see where you're staying?"

"You know, that is a good idea because I would like to take a shower and get out of this monkey suit."

The chauffeur drove us to the hotel. I could not believe it when I walked into Ty's room. We entered the room through a private frosted glass elevator that led right into the living room. His room was three times the size of Aunt Hattie's house, and from it, we had an amazing view of the city. There were chandeliers, mirrored walls, and a master bedroom that was the size of all of our bedrooms *and* the living room *combined.*

"Ty, why is all of this necessary?"

"Well, when you come from humble beginnings like me, anytime I can splurge, I do. But believe it or not, this room is on the house."

"I have never seen anything like this, not even on TV or in the movies."

"Well, make yourself at home. I'm going to take a quick shower."

I looked around and found a fully stocked bar. I had been drinking tequila, so I decided to stick with it. I could hear Chanti saying, "Don't mix your liquor. You won't get too drunk or have a hangover if you don't mix your liquor." So I opened up the bottle of tequila and poured myself two shots back-to-back. I had never really drunk before, but this was making me feel good. Soon, I went back and poured two more shots.

Ty finally came out of the shower in some shorts with a bathrobe on.

"Oooh, can I smell you?"

"Pocahontas, are you okay?"

I stumbled over to him and said, "Yes, I just want to smell you."

As I attempted to sniff his neck, I tripped and fell.

While helping me up, he asked, "Pocahontas, have you been drinking while I was in the shower?"

"Just a little."

He then pulled me to the sofa and told me to have a seat. "I can't take you home like this. Aunt Hattie will be very disappointed in both you and me."

"Who said I wanted to go home?"

"Aunt Hattie, this is Ty. Porchia is really upset, and she has been crying a lot. I came back to my hotel to change clothes, and she fell asleep. Is it okay if I bring her back home after she wakes up?"

"Sure, baby. Just take care of her. Can I trust you to do that?"

"Yes, ma'am. I definitely will. Well, good night."

"Good night, baby."

"See? I told you it would be easy," I slurred.

"Pocahontas, I am really disappointed that you are in this condition."

"Damn it, Ty. Why are you Mr. Goody Two-shoes? I guess you never had too much to drink!"

"We are not talking about me right now."

"Come here, baby. I don't want to argue."

Ty walked over, and I tried to kiss him.

"No, I will not do anything with you when you're in this condition," Ty said while pulling away.

"What? Ty, you don't really like girls."

"No, I don't like girls, especially drunk girls."

"Well, I guess I'll just go get me some more to drink to satisfy my craving."

"No, you will not!" he said sternly. Then he picked me up and took me to the room and started undressing me.

"Yeah, baby, *that's* what I'm talking about," I said.

Then he took me to the bathroom, ran the water, placed me in the shower, and began to bathe me.

****

When I woke up, I was in this humongous bed with a fully clothed Ty lying next to me. I glanced at the clock. It was 1:20 a.m. I panicked, thinking that Aunt Hattie would be worried. Then I remembered that Ty had called her to tell her I would not be coming home, so I drifted back to sleep.

The phone rang, and I looked over at the clock. It was 5:00 a.m. Ty answered it and said, "Thank you."

He then rolled over and said, "How are you feeling this morning, Pocahontas?"

"I'm fine. How are you?" I asked.

"Glad to be lying next to you."

"Ty, do I need to apologize for anything I did last night because I don't remember much."

"Well, you ripped off my clothes, then told me I better do you good or you would kill me."

When I looked at him with a disgusted look on my face, he blurted out, "No, Pocahontas. You pretty much just fell out after I gave you a warm shower."

"Oh no! You saw me naked!"

"Yes, and enjoyed looking at and bathing every inch of your body."

I grabbed the pillow, hit him, and screamed, "Pervert!"

He picked up another pillow and a pillow fight ensued until I collapsed on the bed, and he collapsed on top of me. We began kissing until it got steamy, hot, and passionate. I thought I would explode. I eventually pulled away, not wanting us to go any further. He had such a sad look on his face when I did that.

"I'm sorry, Pocahontas. But my feelings just took over. I love you."

Did he just say the "L" word?

Ty jumped up and said his flight left at 8:30 and asked if I would mind riding with him to the airport. He explained that he wanted to take me home and tell Aunt Hattie and Mystery bye, but he just did not have the time. I told him that it was quite all right. I had no problem going with him to the airport. He scrambled around quickly to get his things together. He, then, jumped in the shower and asked me if I wanted to join him. "For some reason, I feel squeaky clean. But thanks for the offer."

The ride to the airport was sort of quiet. He spent his time checking his messages and doing other things on his phone. I sat thinking about the night and him telling me that he loved me. Ty could have any woman he wanted. I still did not understand why he'd put all of his effort into me. Well, I did not really know what he did when he was away. *He probably has a girlfriend in Birmingham or lots of girlfriends*, I thought. *I've heard about basketball groupies, and, as fine as he is, I know that plenty of women are chasing him. I just don't understand why he's chasing after me.*

"Penny for your thoughts, Pocahontas."

"You will go broke asking about my thoughts."

"I have enough money to spend, so indulge me."

"Ty, do you have a girlfriend?"

"Yes, I do."

My face must have dropped, but it did not seem to stop him. He went on to say, "She is very intelligent, beautiful, athletic, spunky, assertive, funny, and a drunk."

"Ty, I'm serious."

"I'm serious, too. You are my lady, right?"

The driver announced that we had arrived at the terminal, and I could not have been more thankful because I was not ready to answer that question.

Ty looked into my eyes and told me that he'd meant what he said when he said that he loved me, and that he was not going anywhere. He would stay until I figured out that I loved him, too. He kissed me, and then exited the limousine. The minute he closed the door, I felt lost and empty. I wanted to run after him and tell him that I loved him, too, but my legs would not move. I was frozen. I had never been here before and was not certain that I liked being here. I felt more vulnerable than I had ever felt in my life.

Chapter 12

Unbeknownst to me, Ty had made arrangements with the driver to make a detour before taking me home. We arrived at the Galleria, and I asked the driver what was going on. He informed me that he had been instructed by Mr. Gamble to stop and pick up something. The driver came back with a Tiffany and Co. bag. There was a little Tiffany blue box inside. I opened the box and found a white gold diamond tennis bracelet with a note.

The note said: PLEASE ACCEPT THIS GIFT AS A TOKEN OF OUR FLOURISHING RELATIONSHIP. LOVE, TY.

Tears began flowing from my eyes because no one had ever been this generous to me before. But I knew that I could not accept such an expensive gift. In the back of my mind, I wondered, *What is really going on with him? Does Ty have an ulterior motive?* The driver stopped at Aunt Hattie's, and then came around to open my door. I handed him the gift and told him to let Mr. Gamble know I appreciated the thought, but I could not accept the gift.

I walked into the house and could hear that Aunt Hattie was in the shower because she was singing one of her gospel songs. Before I could step into my room, Mystery accosted me, asking me where I had been all night. I was not going to let this tramp ruin my day. Then she went on to say that I was not pulling my weight as it related to taking care of Aunt Hattie. She was working a full-time job, and then had to come home and take care of everything here.

I had to talk myself down because I was about to reach back from New York and brang it back to California to slap this ho. Instead, I said, "Mystery, let me know what you would like for me to do to help out. I am more than willing to put in my fair share."

I, then, walked away and closed my door. *Humph. That felt good!*

I spent Sunday trying to get ready for school the next day. I had seriously been neglecting my studies. My phone rang, and it was Poo Man. I had not heard from him in a while.

"Hey, Poo Boo! What's going on?"

"Hey, Shorty. Why you sounding so happy? Does it have anything to do with my cousin?"

"Nah, Poo Man, I'm just glad to be able to make it to another day without someone dying, killing themselves." I paused, realizing I had dropped myself, "Or anything crazy like that."

Poo Man did not seem to catch on to what I was saying and responded, "Well, the day ain't over with yet."

"Ah, Poo Man, why you gotta try to bring yo' girl down?"

"Nah, Shorty, you know I am just playing with you. I was just checking on you. I'm glad to hear you up."

"No man can keep a good woman down, Poo."

"I hear ya, Shorty. Well, I'm out."

"Lata, Poo Man."

****

After I got out of bed for school, I went and checked on Aunt Hattie.

"Aunt Hattie, would you like anything for breakfast?"

"Baby, can you make me some oatmeal?"

"Is that the only thing on the list you can eat, Aunt Hattie?"

"No, but I like oatmeal."

"Aunt Hattie, you ate biscuits, bacon, eggs, and grits in the morning. I never saw you eat oatmeal."

"And you ain't neva seen me at no hospital either. It is time to eat better, Baby Girl."

"Okay, I got you."

I went to the kitchen to make Aunt Hattie some oatmeal. Mystery came into the kitchen saying, "It's about time you did something around here."

I responded, "Yes, it is."

She walked away, huffing and puffing.

I went to school for the first time in a long time with a little pep in my step. I had a smile on my face and knew that I could make it through this day. I rarely went to the cafeteria for lunch, but I noticed that when I got there, I was getting funny looks. After school, I went to basketball practice, and some of the girls were more standoffish than usual. I asked one of my teammates what was up, and she said she didn't know what I was talking about. I was glad when practice was over because it did not feel right at all. Coach did not even seem as warm as he was normally with me.

When I got home, I chatted with Aunt Hattie's nurse about her condition and the dos and don'ts. Aunt Hattie did not have a lot of restrictions with the exception of lifting heavy objects and engaging in strenuous activity. I told Nurse Leilani that I wanted to get Aunt Hattie to go with me on my daily walk. She thought it was a great idea. Just as I was going to ask Nurse Leilani about the meals, my phone rang. Oh, dang! It was Tracy. I had been meaning to call her.

"Hey, girl."

"Hey, Porchia. How are you?"

"I'm good. What's going on?"

"Nothing. I should be asking you that question."

"What are you talking about, Tracy?"

"Why did you not tell me who Ty was when we were at the hospital?"

"Because I did not know who Ty was when we were at the hospital."

"Well, the talk around town is that you are trying to snatch him up for his money, just like your cousin."

"Trace, you know me. I am *nothing* like Mystery. I did *not* know who Ty was because he did not tell me, nor did he want me to know."

"Porchia, you follow basketball. How could you not know?"

"He looks different from what I knew him to look like. Look, I don't care what everybody is saying. But you're my friend. How could you even think that?"

"I knew better, but I just wanted to let you know what the talk was."

"So is that why everyone at school is acting weird toward me?"

"Probably. But you know I got your back."

"Yeah, I know."

But in the back of my mind I was asking myself, *"Does she?"*

"Porchia, are you going to the dance that the cheerleaders are throwing in honor of Chanti?"

"Probably not, because all of those chicks are fake and never really cared for Chanti in the first place."

"But you did, so you should go and show your respect."

"I'll think about it. I gotta go, Trace."

"Okay, girl, I'll talk with you later."

I looked at my phone because I really needed Ty right now. No one seemed to understand me these days. *I don't have to explain myself or my actions to Ty. He just lets me be me. I need that right now,* I thought. I decided to do my homework to keep my mind off things.

I began straightening out my bed, and my purse fell on the floor and out came Chanti's diary. I'd forgotten all about it. Now I was tempted to read it. Did I want to know Chanti's private thoughts? Did it fall because there was something in there that I needed to know? If our roles had been reversed, would I want her to read my diary? Well, there was not much that she would not already know. I was sure that I knew most things about her, too.

"Oh, what the hell?" I said to myself, and opened the first page of the diary.

Chapter 13

Chanti's diary started off pretty routine, as I thought it would. She wrote a lot of stuff about her fights with her mom. She ranted about her fellow cheerleaders. She talked about me and how she could not have a better friend. She gave her opinion on how she thought I could be dating any guy I wanted but shied away from most people. She questioned one time whether I was really a lesbian. I had to laugh because that kind of took me by surprise. Chanti was the type who would just ask me, "Girl, do you like girls?" She talked a lot about Sweezy and how he should get out of the Life. She dreamed about her future, her loving husband Sweezy, five children, and a house in the suburbs.

At times, I paused and cried. Halfway through the readings, I ran across her discussion with Tracy. Tracy and Chanti were not really friends. They were only friends through me. However, the reading revealed that Tracy had confided in Chanti about being molested at an early age, how this molester was an older relative that everyone trusted. Chanti wrote that she told Tracy that she needed to tell the police or some type of authority figure. According to Chanti's writing, Tracy said that no one would believe her. Chanti wrote about wanting to tell me about it but had given Tracy her word that she would not tell anyone.

Much of Chanti's writing was dedicated to thinking of ways to convince Tracy to go to the police. I stopped there because I could not read anymore.

My mind was racing in so many directions. Should I call Tracy? Should I talk to her dad or her mom? Should I take the book to Child Protective Services to read? I did not know what to do. I wanted to speak with Ty but was not certain if that would be appropriate. I knew I could talk to Aunt Hattie. But she was trying to recover, and I didn't want to burden her with this because of her condition. Dayum! How could their God allow something like this to happen to Tracy? She was the sweetest person that I knew. She would not hurt a fly . . . literally. Tracy did not like hurting insects. She was ghostly afraid of spiders, but when she saw one, she would say, "Don't kill it. Just put it outside." I remember, one time, we were out late, and there were mosquitoes biting us, and she would not slap them but tried to shoo them away. How could their God let something like this happen to her?

I picked up my phone to call Tracy, then decided against it. I needed to think of the proper way to do this. She had never said anything to me or even dropped a clue that she was being molested. I actually thought she was a virgin like me because she never spoke about boys in that way. I decided to text her and ask her if she wanted to have lunch with me tomorrow. We had not spent any time together lately. She texted back that she had to compete in a history competition tomorrow during lunch, but she would be available during lunch on Wednesday.

Dayum! I did not want to have to wait another day, but I guess I had no other choice. I believed Chanti had spoken from the grave and wanted me to know this about Tracy.

"Girl, why are you messing with me from the great beyond? Ain't there something better for you to do in that place they call heaven?" I asked her.

Then I picked up my phone and dialed Ty's number.

"Hi, Ty."

"Pocahontas, we just had a breakthrough. This is the first time you have called me!"

"I was just thinking about you and wondering how it's going for you."

"What's wrong, Pocahontas?"

"Nothing!" I exclaimed. "I just wanted to hear my boyfriend's voice."

"Oh, is this the same boyfriend whose gift you would not accept?"

"Ty, that was entirely too expensive and inappropriate. I would feel like Mystery if I accepted that from you."

Ty laughed. "Yeah, I've heard about your cousin. Heard she is hella of a stripper. Probably the highest paid in Houston."

"She ain't nothing but a broke-down ho."

"Pocahontas, you know I don't like you speaking like that, especially about family."

"I'm just keepin' it 100."

"Well, keep it 100, and tell me what's up."

How is he reading me like this? We are on the phone, and he knows something is wrong.

"Well, I just need to run this scenario by you."

"Okay, I am listening."

I went on to tell him about Chanti's diary. I told him that a friend, without revealing the name, was being molested by a relative. I went on to say that she had not told anybody, not even me. She asked Chanti not to say anything either. Ty sighed before saying anything.

"Pocahontas, that is a very touchy subject, but I know that your friend needs someone to talk to about it. You should bring it up to her while also providing professional resources that she can contact to help her through this issue. She'll need support from you during this time."

"Ty, I'm scared. I'm scared that she might reject what I'm saying. I'm scared that she might not trust me. I'm scared that she'll pull away from me."

"You have to take that chance, Pocahontas. I can tell you that she is in need of a true friend."

"Ty, what did I do to deserve you?"

Ty laughed and said, "Stole that ball from me on the court in front of a whole bunch of dudes."

"Well, I must say that you are a very gracious loser."

"No, I'm just biding my time until I can get back at you."

"Give it up. I can't help it if you play like someone's grandma."

"Yeah, someone's grandma that's pulling in millions."

"If your head gets any bigger, it won't be able to fit in the arena!"

"But you love me."

"Yes, I love you."

"Wow! Did I just get an admission?"

"I'm just showing my appreciation for the support you have given me."

"I will take that, Pocahontas."

"Well, Ty, I have some more homework to do, so I'll holla atcha lata."

"Good night, Love. It was nice hearing from you."

"Good night, Ty."

Can't Nobody

Chapter 14

I was patiently trying to get through my day because, the faster Tuesday passed, the quicker Wednesday would arrive. *How can Tracy be carrying something like this around for years?* I wondered. I was not certain about the signs of sexual abuse, but she appeared to be a regular child growing up and was definitely a regular teenage girl. So what that she did not have any boyfriends and dressed sort of homely? After all, she was a preacher's child. And I was just like her and had not been abused.

After school, I could not do basketball practice, so I went to speak with Coach. Coach told me he understood that I had been going through a lot lately, but he needed my head there. He also told me a couple of scouts had been calling about me, so I probably needed to step up my game. After our discussion, I stayed for practice. We had a good practice, but I still did not seem to have my head in the game. Usually, basketball took my mind away from all that was happening, but today it only increased my anxiety.

I rushed home after practice and found Dr. Dumb sitting and talking with Aunt Hattie and Mystery.

"Hello, everyone. Doctor, I did not realize a doctor of your pedigree made house calls. Or is this something special?"

"Well, hello, Porchia. I just wanted to come and check in on my favorite patient."

"Doctor, you are spoiling me," said Aunt Hattie.

"Yeah, the good doctor has a way of spoiling people," I said.

Mystery looked at me and asked, "Porchia, how was school?"

"I'm glad that you're taking such an interest in me, Mystery. School was fine."

"Let me get out of your way so you all can carry on your business."

"Porchia, honey, Mystery cooked dinner for you. I noticed that you have not been eating right lately. So go on and grab you some food," said Aunt Hattie.

No way, no telling what she'd put in the food if she prepared it for me. There was no love lost between the two of us.

"Thanks, Aunt Hattie, but I ate before I came home. I need to do some homework."

"Porchia, some mail came in for you. I put it on the kitchen counter," said Mystery.

I went to the kitchen and found a letter from Stanford University. I opened it, wondering why they were sending me a letter. I skipped right to and stopped at, "This is a letter of pre-admission to Stanford University with a full academic and athletic scholarship . . ."

I started screaming and yelling. Aunt Hattie came running first, followed by Mystery and Dr. Fine, asking, "What's wrong, Baby Girl?"

"I have been offered a full scholarship to Stanford!"

Dr. Fine said, "That's my alma mater. Congratulations, Porchia! Do you mind if I look at the letter?"

I was so happy because Stanford was my school of choice after Georgetown. I eagerly handed the letter to Dr. Fine.

He said, "This is great, Porchia, but the letter has some additional requirements related to your academic standing. Make sure you read it all, so you can understand what you have to do to be admitted."

"I will, Doctor Little," I eagerly responded.

Aunt Hattie said, "This is a time for celebration. Let's break out the Martinelli sparkling cider and have a toast."

Mystery went to the cabinet for some glasses while I grabbed the sparkling cider. Dr. Fine asked permission from Aunt Hattie to do the toast, and she agreed.

Dr. Fine raised his glass and said, "To good health, great grades, and lasting love."

Oh, hell! Here goes Dr. Dumb with this love thang he thinks he has for Mystery, I thought. Our glasses clinked, and, at that moment, everything seemed like it could get back on track.

I left the group in the kitchen, thinking I needed to call Chanti and tell her the good news. The moment of happiness quickly turned into a feeling of eternal grimness. Then, Tracy came to mind. *How could I celebrate when my friend needed me?* I wondered. I was acting like Mystery at this moment—thinking of no one but myself. I could not even share the good news with Ty. I must concentrate on helping Tracy. I had lost one friend, and I couldn't lose another.

My phone rang, and it was Poo Man. He certainly had been calling me a lot lately.

"Hey, Poo Man! What's up?"

"Turn on your TV to Channel 13 News!"

"What's going on?" I asked as I looked for the remote.

"Turn it on now!"

I finally found the remote and turned on the television, and I could not believe what I was seeing. Ms. Carletta was being led away from her house in handcuffs by the HPD.

"Poo Man, what's going on?"

"They said that she shot and killed Pastor Charles!"

"What? Poo Man, I gotta go!"

I ran to the kitchen and saw that Aunt Hattie, Dr. Dumb, and the Tramp were still having a cozy discussion around the table. I felt as if I was interrupting something.

"Aunt Hattie, I forgot that I was supposed to help Tracy with some schoolwork. I'll be gone for a little bit."

"Okay, Baby Girl. Be careful out there."

"I will."

I bent down to kiss her and said farewell to the doctor. I hated lying to Aunt Hattie, but in her condition, I could not yet let her know what was going on. She would be worried and really could not do anything about the matter now. Plus, I needed to find out what happened. It made no sense that Ms. Carletta would kill her husband. She worshiped the ground that man walked on, and I hoped that Tracy was holding it together with everything that she was going through.

****

When I got to the house, the police were still there and were not letting anyone into the house. They had placed the yellow crime scene tape all around. I took out my phone to call Tracy. The call went to voice mail right away. I knew that the officers probably had the house surrounded, but I decided to check the back entrance. To my surprise, no one was at the door. I pulled the door, and it opened. I could hear voices in the living room. I heard noise coming from her oldest brother's room off the kitchen. I peeped in and could see that the girls were watching cartoons. The boys were playing on a game system. I quickly tried to bypass them so I could go to Tracy's room. Just as I passed the children's room, my phone rang. It was Mystery.

What in the hell does she want? I quickly answered it, trying to make certain the kids did not hear me.

"Porchia, we just heard that Ms. Carletta killed Pastor Charles. Were you over there when it happened?"

I whispered, "No, I was not. I just arrived."

"Well, what happened?"

"I don't know. I am waiting to speak with Tracy."

"Aunt Hattie is about to have another heart attack over here. She's walking around saying, 'Oh, Jesus' over and over again."

"Mystery, you and the doctor take care of Aunt Hattie. I need to be with Tracy right now."

"Well, when you find out what happened, call me."

Yeah, well, she's gonna have to hold her breath on that one, I thought.

"Okay," I said and hung up.

I was walking in the direction of Tracy's room, and I could see that entire section of the house was sectioned off. I was just about to go back to her oldest brother's room when Tracy appeared in the hallway.

"Porchia, what are you doing here? And how did you get past all of the officers?"

"I had to come check on you after I heard what happened. Are you okay?"

"Porchia, I really don't want to talk about any of this. I need to tend to the kids."

"I can stay and help, and then we can talk when you're done."

"My grandmother and aunt are on their way to help me."

"Your grandmother?"

"Yes, they called as soon as they heard the news."

"Look, Trace, you don't have to talk about anything. I just want to be with you as your friend."

"I'm okay. I promise, but I won't be able to have lunch with you tomorrow."

"Oh, I understand. We can have lunch another day. Is there anything that I can do for you before I leave?"

"No, Porchia. Thanks for coming."

"I'm here for you, and, if you need anything or just feel like talking, call me day or night."

"I know, girl."

I hugged Tracy and reluctantly left the same way I'd come in. Tracy was unusually calm, considering her mother had been hauled off to jail and her father was dead.

Can't Nobody

Chapter 15

I felt so helpless. I did not know what I could do to help Tracy. I couldn't believe that her grandmother, who she had been estranged from for all of these years, was about to come over to help. Tracy barely knew who she was and the younger kids definitely did not know her.

I walked into my house, and Aunt Hattie was sitting, rocking in her chair. She looked distraught, and, when she saw me, she jumped up and said, "Porchia, what happened? Is what we heard really true? Did Sister Carletta *really* kill Pastor Charles? Tell me, child, that this is not true."

"I'm sorry, Aunt Hattie," I said.

"What happened, Baby Girl?"

"I don't know. I could not speak with Tracy."

"Oh, Lawd, please reach out and help the family right now! How are the kids?"

"They seemed to be okay. I'm not certain they know what is going on. Aunt Hattie, I need for you to not get worked up. I will do whatever I can to help. I need for you to take care of yourself. I would not be able to stand another person leaving me."

Although I never really cared for Pastor Charles because he seemed like the ultimate pimp in my opinion, I knew that Aunt Hattie loved both him and

Ms. Carletta, and I was seriously concerned about Aunt Hattie having a relapse. I was happy when I finally convinced her to go lie down.

While she rested, I walked around the house, nervously cleaning up and moving things around. My phone rang, and I ran to it, thinking it might be Tracy.

"Pocahontas, it's all over the news that Pastor Charles was killed by that sweet lady I met in Aunt Hattie's room. What happened?"

"Hi, Ty. I don't know."

"Well, have you spoken with your friend?"

"I tried, but she wouldn't talk. Ty, I didn't tell you, but the friend I was talking about earlier was Tracy. I know this is too much for her. I don't know what I can do, but I feel I need to do something!"

"The best thing you can do is be there for her when she wants to talk. Don't push it, Pocahontas. She'll open up when she's ready."

"I can't just sit back, Ty! She's the only friend I have left."

"You have me!"

"Thanks, Ty. And I'm glad that you are here for me."

"As long as you allow me to be here, I'll be here."

"Ty, let me call you back. The news is coming on."

"Okay, call me back later."

The news just reported the same thing that I already knew. They reported that Ms. Carletta was in custody and that there was an ongoing investigation into the death of Pastor Charles. Ms. Carletta's sister was interviewed, and she asked for the media to give the family their privacy during this very difficult time. The news showed various people from the neighborhood who said that they could not believe that this was happening to this family. Why does the media always find the most ignorant black person to speak to when something happens? The man speaking could not put two words together! I turned off the news, realizing that I would not get any more information than I already had.

I needed to speak to Tracy, but she was probably still avoiding me.

"Trace! I was not expecting you to answer. How are you?"

"We're okay. We're staying with my grandparents. Their home is spectacular. You should see this place."

"Trace, what happened?"

"I can't talk, Porchia. I've been asked not to say anything."

"Who told you that?"

"My grandparents. I have to go. I'll be in contact soon."

Tracy hung up the phone as quickly as she had answered it. I had to wonder what her grandparents were telling her. How could Tracy trust them after they had pretty much abandoned them for all of these years?

I thought about calling Ty back but was exhausted from the day's events. Instead, I decided to take a hot bath. After getting out of the tub, I checked on Aunt Hattie. She was knocked out. I needed something to calm me down, so I listened to some Rachelle Ferrell. Most kids my age had not even heard of her, but she was one of the rawest singers I'd ever heard. I sat back, listened to "With Open Arms," and let the tears just flow from my eyes.

I missed Chanti so much right now, and nothing could help me with the pain that I was feeling. We could have worked through this "Tracy thing" together. *Humph, God!* How could there be a God? Doesn't anyone else see that if there *is* a God, He is cruel? Does He just go around pulling strings and determining what happens to whom and when? I refuse to be His puppet!

****

I woke up the next morning with my headphones still on my ears. The last thing I remembered was listening to Rachelle and Will Downing sing "Nothing Has Ever Felt like This." I'd gone to sleep thinking about Ty. I wished I could just sleep the day away because I was not ready to face all of those fake people at school. Independent study was looking more and more like the thing for me. But I was not certain that I would remain in my AP courses if I opted to do it by independent study. I didn't want anything to interfere with my ability to go to Stanford or perhaps Georgetown.

I arrived at school right after the first bell and had to hurry to make it to chemistry before the second bell. Just my luck, we were having a pop quiz today. I had not been putting as much time as I should into my studies. I struggled through the quiz and knew I had failed. Before leaving the classroom, Mr. Papal, who served as my chemistry teacher and academic advisor, stopped me and asked me if I could meet him during lunch in his office. I thought, *Damn! I know I have been messing up, but there is a reason.*

"Sure, Mr. Papal."

"Thanks, Porchia. I'll see you at lunch."

My mind was really not on my class since Mr. Papal wanted to speak with me. What type of bad news would he be delivering to me today?

Lunch could not have come fast enough. I walked briskly to Mr. Papal's office. On the way into his office, I saw Principal Ashton, and he asked me to stop in his office on the way out of Mr. Papal's office. *Oh, damn! I am on a roll today. Getting it from all ends!*

"Yes, sir."

My heart began racing, and I started feeling faint and dizzy. I could see all of my dreams vanishing before me. What could he have to say to me?

"Hello, Mr. Papal."

"Hi, Porchia. Please shut the door behind you."

Oh no, this is going to be worse than I thought!

"Mr. Papal, before you start, I must let you know that I have been under a lot of pressure lately. I know my grades are not what you would expect from me, but I will concentrate on my studies to make certain I land a scholarship. I just received a letter from Stanford University, offering me a conditional acceptance, and I am going to do everything in my power to ensure that I do what is necessary."

"Porchia. Porchia. Please take a breath. I am not here to reprimand you about your grades."

"I'm sorry, Mr. Papal. I don't understand."

"Well, we have been looking at your credits, courses, and your grades and wanted to tell you that you can graduate this year if you take Intermediate and Advanced Spanish at the same time next semester."

My mouth dropped wide open, and I exclaimed, "What?"

"Yes, ma'am, and, if you keep it up, you will be graduating with the highest honors from this year's graduating class."

Mr. Papal went on and said, "We also have been contacted by Georgetown to nominate a student who would be interested in attending their university on a full academic scholarship. Additionally, they are offering a position working with one of the most prestigious biochemical researchers at the university. They are particularly interested in inner-city students with high academic standings. I am here to find out if you would be interested in this opportunity."

I wanted to say yes, but nothing was coming from my mouth. Mr. Papal went on to say, "It would not allow you the opportunity to play basketball because much of your time will be with studies and researching."

"Yes! Yes! Yes! I can't believe this. Are you sure I would be eligible if I took both of my Spanish courses simultaneously?"

"Yes, I have conferred with your other teachers, and they have assured me that your grades are up to par so far. I have looked over all of the requirements, and you are definitely qualified."

I jumped up and grabbed Mr. Papal, holding him so tight he began gasping for air.

"I am so sorry, but this is the best news I have heard in a long time. Is there anything that I would be required to pay for?"

"No, Porchia, in addition to tuition, books, and room and board, you will be getting a stipend from the university that will cover any additional expenses that you might have."

"Mr. Papal, I just flunked the quiz you gave us."

He laughed and said, "No worries, my child."

"Thanks, Mr. Papal."

"Just don't let me down, Porchia."

"I won't, sir."

"I expect you to do big things."

As I walked out of his office, Principal Ashton was standing there, grinning like a Cheshire cat.

"So are congratulations in order?"

"Mr. Ashton, how long have you known about this?"

"I just learned day before yesterday, but I could not think of anyone more deserving than you, Porchia. I know you have gone through a lot lately, but you have a lot to look forward to. Sister Hattie will be so happy and so proud."

"Mr. Ashton, it will be difficult leaving her in Mystery's hands."

He laughed and replied, "I'm certain Mystery can handle it. It's time for you to think about your life and what you deserve, young lady."

Although I knew this was good news, once I started walking home, I realized it was bittersweet. I would be leaving Aunt Hattie and Tracy. And I would be further away from Ty. I loved playing basketball, but it was more of a pastime for me. It was a means of escape from my everyday life. It didn't matter whether I played at the collegiate level or not. I had no intention of playing professionally.

As a matter of fact, it was comforting to know that I would not have to play ball in order to go to school. I could concentrate on my studies and the career that I wanted. I wanted to make certain that my life on earth counted. Even if I didn't believe in God or the afterlife, I believed that everyone should make his or her life meaningful in some way. My quest was to dedicate my life to fighting diseases like cancer that kills millions of people daily. I could ensure that children did not lose their parents to this nasty disease. I could ensure that mothers did not lose their kids to this nasty disease. I would be able to fulfill my purpose through this opportunity.

Chapter 16

I walked home excited and ready to share my news with Aunt Hattie. When I opened the door, Mystery was jumping up and down and laughing with Aunt Hattie.

"What the heck is going on here?" I asked.

"I'z getting married," responded Mystery, flaunting the shiny, big diamond ring that Dr. Dumb had shown me at the hospital.

"Dr. Dumb went through with it I see," I blurted.

"What?" said Mystery.

"So I see you finally sucked one in."

"Damn it, Porchia! Why can't you just be happy about something that happens to me one day in your life? You are a cruel ingrate! And I am so tired of you and your attitude!"

Aunt Hattie grabbed her heart and said, "Oh no! I think this might be the big one!"

I immediately ran to her, and Mystery stopped in the middle of her ranting.

"Ha-ha! Remember when Fred Sanford would say that all the time," said Aunt Hattie while cracking up.

I looked at her and scornfully said, "Aunt Hattie, don't ever do that again! That is not funny."

"What is not funny is you two arguing all of the time. You are making my heart ache. It needs to stop today!" she exclaimed.

I just looked at both of them, shook my head, and then walked away.

I could not share my news with them, so I called Ty. My phone call went to voice mail, so I left a message for him to call me as soon as he received the message. I turned on the television and caught a special bulletin announcing that Ms. Carletta had been released from jail on a $500,000 bond. I had to wonder who had enough money to bail her out. Perhaps her family had come to her rescue.

I wanted to call Tracy but knew she probably would still not want to talk with me. My mind quickly switched to my conversation with Mr. Papal. Now that I knew that I would be graduating next semester, I wanted to ensure that I passed all of my tests with flying colors. Despite everything that was happening around me, I now had something to strive for. Although I wanted to make sure Tracy was okay, I wouldn't obsess over it because I needed to concentrate on my studies.

****

My morning classes went well. I actually had not done that bad on my chemistry quiz. I only missed one problem, which put me at an A-. During lunch, I touched base with Coach to tell him what was going on. He told me that they really would like to have me play for the entire season, but he understood if I decided to concentrate on my studies. I told him I would get back to him by tomorrow with my decision, but today I would practice with the team. It was great being out there with the team, and it actually took my mind off what was going on around me.

I joined some of my teammates for pizza after practice. Our season was starting next week, so they thought we could celebrate before the season started. Tyra was the person on the team that I clicked with the most.

"Are you going to the dance, Porchia?" she asked.

"I'm still thinking about it."

"I am so sorry about what happened to your friend. Every time I saw her, she was smiling. She had such a good vibe."

"Yeah, Chanti was pretty special."

After our pizza arrived, I stayed another hour, just kicking it with my teammates. Everyone was pretty hyped about our first game because we were playing against the champions we'd lost to last year. I looked at my phone and noticed that I had missed a call from an unknown number. There was a message. Excited to see what Ty said, I excused myself from the crew and told them I would see them tomorrow. As I departed, I decided that I would remain with the team for the season.

"Hi, Pocahontas. Sorry I was not able to talk with you last night. We had a late practice. But I heard excitement in your voice. I hope you have some good news, like you are coming to visit me soon. I miss you. Call me back. Love ya!"

Hearing Ty say he loved me gave me chills. I still was not comfortable with him saying it. I knew that I thought of him throughout the day. I knew just the thought of him made me smile. When he was in my presence, I did not want him to leave. I knew that, when he touched me, I got goose bumps. I didn't know if that was love, but whatever I was feeling, it sure felt good.

The house was empty when I arrived. I thought I would get my homework out of the way because I wanted to spend some time talking with Ty. Aunt Hattie and Mystery came through the door two hours later. I did not realize I had spent that much time on my homework. I had an English assignment that was kicking my butt. I didn't mind math and science, but the liberal arts were not my best.

"Hey, Baby Girl! How was school?" Aunt Hattie asked.

I realized I had not told her about my plans but did not have time to do it right now.

"Fine, Aunt Hattie. And how was your day?"

"Mystery and I went to visit Ms. Carletta in jail."

I came to a complete stop and ran out of my room.

"So, Aunt Hattie, what did she say?"

"She said that the district attorney offered her a plea bargain. She and her lawyer will discuss it tomorrow."

"Aunt Hattie, did she say why she killed Pastor Charles?"

"She said it was an accident, but she will not able to talk about it until after the case is over."

"Did she look sad?"

"Baby Girl, she looked bad! I asked her if there was anything we could do for her or the kids. She told me that her mother and father were taking care of the kids."

This entire situation was odd to me. It was as if Ms. Carletta, because of Pastor Charles's death, had an instant connection back to her parents. As I remembered, the family had told her that they never wanted to see her again. I believe their words were: "You and your children are dead to us." How could there be such a big change in attitude? I wondered if her folks had anything to do with the accidental death of Pastor Charles. I did not like the man, but no one deserved to be killed just because he was not liked. I decided that I'd give Tracy another day before I contacted her again.

My phone rang with an unknown number, and I became excited because I knew it was Ty. *Humph! He can't wait for me to call him back.*

"Hi! Is this Porchia Williams?"

"Who is this?"

"You don't need to know that, but I have some information for you."

"What makes you think that I care about any information that an unknown person has for me?"

"Do you care about Tracy?"

"What does this have to do with Tracy?"

"You share more with Tracy than you think."

"What are you talking about? Will you just tell me? Or will you just play like you are the Riddler?"

"I think I have said enough. You are going to have to work through the rest yourself."

"Look, I don't appreciate you calling me, playing games. Don't do me any more favors."

I hit the end button. The phone rang back with an unknown number again.

"Look. Don't fucking call my phone again!"

"Pocahontas?"

"Oh, sorry, Ty. I thought you were somebody else."

"Would you care to talk about it?"

Chapter 17

I talked with Ty into the wee hours of the morning. He was supportive about me leaving school early to attend Georgetown but was surprised to learn that I did not want to play ball. He asked me to take my time before making a final decision. He, also, told me that there were a lot of sick people in the world who liked to prey on people when they were at their most vulnerable. And again, he asked me to come and visit him in Birmingham. He ended the conversation by advising me to be careful about the people I trusted. That was one thing that I did not need to be warned about because, at that point in my life, the only person I trusted was Aunt Hattie. Little did he know, he was still on the suspect list.

I continued going through the motions of daily life, just waiting for the semester to end. My grades were exceptional. The basketball team was on fire and unbeatable that year. The team was introduced with our theme song, "Turn Down for What," at all of our home games. When we were at away games, we came out stomping and chanting the song.

Scouts continued to come to our games, looking at me and Keisha, the shooting guard on our team. She averaged 20 points a game, and I was responsible for directing the team's offense with my record-breaking assists. Although I turned it up every game, it was more about the team and Coach because I knew that I was headed to Georgetown but thought I would keep my options open.

Aunt Hattie was recovering well while Mystery was out of my way because she was busy planning her wedding. Ms. Carletta accepted a plea bargain and was put on probation. The entire family was staying with Ms. Carletta's parents.

I did not see much of Tracy anymore because she'd started attending private school on the other side of town. I went to visit her at her grandparents' once, and it seemed like all was well. We spoke regularly on the phone, and Tracy, in my opinion, sounded happier than she had in a long time. She had less responsibility at her grandparents' and could enjoy the things that teenagers should enjoy.

Ty's popularity had increased substantially since he'd begun playing pro ball. He had problems now doing everyday things like grocery shopping or getting gas. His life seemed like it was extra busy. Despite his season and popularity, Ty and I spoke almost every day. Ty was my support system through everything that I encountered. He continued to ask me to visit him, and, with everything going so well, I decided it was time to take him up on his offer.

I headed off to Birmingham in a sullen mood because we had lost our first game of the season. No one was on their game, especially me. Ty told me that a driver would be there to pick me up and would have my name on a card when I reached the baggage claim. I saw a handsome man dressed in a black suit holding a sign that read "Pocahontas." I could not have been more embarrassed. I thought about not going up to him, but was not certain of another way to get to Ty since I did not have his address. When we reached the limousine, Ty was in the limo with rose petals spread all over the seat, a bottle of sparkling cider, and the biggest grin I had ever seen. Oooh, those pearly white teeth and those dimples killed me every time.

As I was entering the limo, he grabbed me, laid me down, and passionately kissed me.

Gasping for air when he let me up, I panted, "Oh, I see you missed me."

"No, just trying to make you forget about that win you gave to Sterling last night."

"Ty, you are cruel!"

"I'm sorry, Pocahontas," Ty said, putting his hands in a praying position. "Will you let me make it up to you?"

I laughed, knowing that he was not really being apologetic.

As the driver drove us around, we chatted about the things that happened since we had last spoken, which was only a day ago. Ty and I drove up to a restaurant where we were quickly escorted to a private room. There, we were served a seven-course meal, and it did not seem like the food would ever stop coming. I thought I was full, but, by the time dessert came, they had a rum-soaked bread pudding that I could not resist.

Ty refused dessert and said he would only like coffee. "Ty, you love bread pudding. Why are you not eating it?"

"I do want my dessert," he said, licking his full lips . . . "just a little later."

I wish he would not do things like that because now I was feeling my legs getting sticky!

Ty lived in this area called Mountain Brook, which was a suburb of Birmingham. As we drove up to his place, I thought, *What a waste of space! This is entirely too big for one person.*

When we pulled up, he just smiled, while reading my mind, and said, "C'mon, Pocahontas. I have also been giving to charities."

"Ty, this is too much."

"Says who?"

"Says yo' woman!"

He sighed and said, "Well, she'll get used to it."

"Who cleans this place?"

"I was hoping that you would do some cleaning while you were here."

I rolled my eyes and said, "Whateva."

We walked through the house, and the ceilings looked like they were thirty feet high. It was just so extreme that I stopped and stared at him, then looked back at the room. It did not get better. The dining room had a 22-seat table with an extraordinary chandelier. The living room had a white grand piano with all white furniture, accenting the room. The media room contained a mini movie theater. The game room had all sorts of games, including foosball, ping pong, billiards, darts, and several old-school video game consoles like Asteroids, Galaga, and Pac Man.

Ty gave me a thirty-minute tour of the house, which also included an inside basketball court, a full gym, and a swimming pool. Not to mention, there was an outside tennis court, racquet ball court, and a basketball court with an Olympic-size swimming pool. To say I was overwhelmed by it all was a serious understatement.

"I know, Pocahontas. It looks big right now, but you'll get used to it."

"Ty, I could never get used to all of this."

"Let me show you our room."

Ty's bedroom was unlike the rest of the house. It had a warm, cozy feeling, although it was humongous. It was decorated with earth tones. There was a step-down Jacuzzi that was about six feet from his bed. The room accommodated a large sectional sofa to watch his 120-inch TV that was built into the wall with surround sound speakers. Ty also had a combination sitting room/office off his bedroom. His bathroom included a shower built for ten people with jets and showerheads coming from all directions. There was also a soaking Jacuzzi tub that could comfortably accommodate eight large adults.

"Ty, are there kinky things going on here or something? Why is your shower and tub so big?"

"Pocahontas, it was here when I got here, and I like it. Plus, I would like to do some kinky things with you in the shower and bathtub."

"Forget that, dude. I don't know who you have been with in there!"

Ty cozied up to me and nibbled on my ear and said, "But we can make new memories together."

I shoved him away and said, "Only in your dreams, buddy."

****

Ty and I watched a few movies before I fell asleep in his arms. He woke me up and told me to get in bed.

"Where is my bedroom?" I asked.

"Pocahontas, we won't do anything that you don't want to do. Your place is with me."

"Well, I would like to take a shower."

"Mi casa es su casa."

The driver had put the bags downstairs, so Ty went and brought my bags up. I actually had gone shopping because I could not wear T-shirts to bed with Ty. I found a couple of cute nighties and was trying to decide which one I was going to wear when Ty walked in and said, "I like that one."

"Your vote does not count, mister."

However, I took that one into the bathroom.

I stepped into the shower and could not figure out how to operate it.

"Ty! What do I do to take a shower?"

Ty walked in and explained how to operate it. There were buttons for music and lights. I accidently turned on the rain forest water head and wet all of my hair. I screamed, and Ty came running in asking what was wrong. When I told him I'd wet my hair, he said, "No problem. I'll call a hairstylist tomorrow to fix it up."

"Ty, that is ridiculous. I can wash and blow-dry my own hair."

"Okay, suit yourself."

I got out of the shower and attempted to towel dry my hair because I did not feel like blow-drying it. Once dressed in my nightie, I went into the room, and Ty was already in bed without a shirt. I looked at his ripped chest and prayed that he, at least, had on shorts.

He looked at me and said, "Hurry up, Pocahontas. I've been waiting for this a long time. By the way, you look sexy with your curly hair."

I looked at him, disgusted, and said, "Ty, I am not ready to have sex."

"'I' not looking for sex either. I'm just looking to hold you close to me."

I jumped on top of him, and he said, "Girl, don't play with me."

He body slammed me on his bed, then got on top of me, and pinned my hands up above my head. I struggled to get away from him but could not.

He said, "Say 'uncle,' and I'll let you up."

"I am not saying 'uncle' to you!"

After struggling for two minutes, I shouted, "Uncle!"

"Yes, Pocahontas, you have to learn who is in control here."

I started kissing his neck, and he became like putty in my hand. "Yes, Ty, I learned a long time ago that women are always in control."

He caught my face and began gently kissing my cheeks, then my forehead, then moved down to my chin, and finally found his way to my mouth. *Mmm . . . His kisses feel so good.* I began panting. Ty moved back down to my chin and then proceeded to my neck. He went to my neck, then down to my chest, and used his tongue to flirt around my breasts. Oh! He teased me until I whimpered, "Ty, please suck my breasts."

"Yes, ma'am." Ty gently sucked my left breast while taking his hand and gently circling his fingers on my right breast. He rotated from breast to breast for a while.

He then moved down and kissed my stomach. He played around my navel, and moved south. I softly grunted and said, "No."

Ty began to come back up and play with my navel again, then back up to my breasts. I could feel that I was getting wetter and wetter and hoped I was not wetting his sheets, which felt like nothing I had ever felt before.

I was lost in the moment, and before I knew it, Ty had opened my legs, and his tongue was darting on my clit. I thought I would explode at that moment. I no longer resisted and allowed him to do whatever he was doing down there. I think I must have come because my whole body began shaking and convulsing, and I felt a wave of pleasure that I had never felt before. Ty came back up, kissing my stomach, and eventually worked his way back to my lips.

"So did you enjoy that?"

"Ty, you know I have never been with a guy, right?"

"Yes, Pocahontas, I know."

"So what just happened?" I asked.

"From all of the wetness I felt, I would bet my last dime that you had an orgasm."

He put on a condom, and the night of lovemaking continued because I could not get enough. I think Ty came at least three times, and I came another four times. I was so glad that I had never experienced this before because I would have definitely indulged in this pleasure more often.

Now, I completely understood what Chanti was talking about when she talked about sex. For the remainder of my stay in Birmingham, Ty and I mainly stayed in bed, making love. We only came up for air, water, and food. Between our lovemaking sessions, I confessed to him that I loved him. Ty and I confirmed that we were committed to each other. He gave me a key to his home and told me that anytime I wanted to come, whether he was there or not, I was free to do so.

Can't Nobody

Chapter 18

I could not stop thinking about Ty for the entire plane ride home. I started contemplating whether the University of Alabama could be my college of choice. I had not researched their programs nor had I ever thought about going to school in Alabama. Living in Houston was as much of the South that I would like to experience. When I thought of Alabama, I thought of George Wallace and the bombing that killed the four young girls in church. I knew Houston may have its problems, but discrimination did not seem to run as deep as it did in Alabama.

My thoughts were interrupted by an announcement from the captain for everyone to make certain their seat belts were buckled and for the flight attendants to suspend service and take their seats. Within seconds, the plane started violently shaking, and items flew from the overhead bins. People started screaming, and the flight attendants scrambled for their seats.

After experiencing the violent shaking and dipping for about two minutes, the captain came on the speaker and apologized for the unexpected turbulence. The remainder of the plane ride was extremely quiet. My stomach was upside down by the time we arrived at Intercontinental. I was not certain that I would be making many more trips to Alabama on a plane.

Mystery picked me up at the airport. She was in a peculiarly good mood. When she first saw me, she reached out and hugged me.

"So, Porchia, did you enjoy your time in Alabama?"

"It was okay."

"Where does Ty live, and what is his place like?"

"He lives a few miles outside of the city, and his house is okay."

"Porchia, I have a very important question to ask you."

"What?"

"Are you on birth control pills?"

"What the hell, Mystery? What business is it of yours?"

"I just don't want anything interfering with our plans. Everything is on track right now. I am marrying the man of my dreams. He is building me my dream house. Aunt Hattie is doing well. She'll be moving in with us, and I can take care of her full-time. You are headed to college. What else could we ask for?"

"Sounds like you don't want me interfering with your plans. Don't worry. I don't want to live with you."

"That is not it, Porchia. I want you to be happy! Since you were a little girl, you talked about going to college."

"Mystery, do me a favor and just don't talk to me."

"Well, I have a favor to ask of you."

"I am all out of favors when it comes to you."

Mystery just ignored my comment and asked, "Would you be my maid of honor?"

Silence.

"Well, you don't have to answer me now. Just think about it."

Does this tramp ever stop with her antics? What would make her think that I would ever stand up next to her? When we got home, I ran into the house in search of Aunt Hattie. She was in the kitchen cooking when I ran up behind her and gave her a big bear hug.

"Well, Baby Girl, I'm happy to see you, too," she chirped.

"Aunt Hattie, should you be cooking?"

"Chile, I can't eat anymore of Mystery's cooking. So, yes, I should be cooking."

"Did you miss me?"

"Yes, I did, but I did not miss those walks you force me to go on," she said, huffing.

"Ah, come on, Aunt Hattie! You know you enjoy our walks. I am going to put my stuff down, and then we can go for a walk."

"No, Baby Girl, not today. We are having a meeting over here to decide what to do about getting a new minister."

"Try not to pick a pimp this time."

"Porchia!"

"I'm just teasing, Aunt Hattie," I said, kissing her on her cheek.

"I need to catch up on my studies. I'll be in my room."

"Okay, Baby Girl, but the food is almost ready, so you can eat before they come."

"Thanks, Aunt Hattie."

I called Ty to let him know that I had made it safely. We had a short conversation because some of the players were at his house. I tried to dive into my schoolwork, but my mind kept drifting back to Ty. My thoughts were interrupted by the doorbell ringing. I thought I heard Principal Ashton arrive with another deacon and his wife. Within a few moments, I could hear a lot of chatter. I put on my headphones, so I could concentrate on something other than the discussion coming from the group.

After several hours of doing work, I had to use the bathroom. I took off my headphones and noticed that the chattering had stopped.

I was headed to the bathroom when I heard an unfamiliar voice say, "Well, they pretty much let Sister Carletta go because she walked in on Pastor Charles on top of their eldest daughter. She lost her head, got a pistol from the drawer, and shot him in the back."

Aunt Hattie asked, "Are you sure?"

The voice said, "Yes, and you know Sister Carletta's brother works for the district attorney? She probably will not do any time, even if she shot him in cold blood!"

Another voice said, "Well, that bastard got exactly what he deserved if he was sexually abusing his daughter!"

I could not listen anymore.

I felt sick to my stomach. I ran to the bathroom and started throwing up. All of this time, I thought it was a relative. I had no idea it was her good-for-nothing, pimping father! I probably would have tried to kill him myself if I had known. What type of permanent damage had he done to his own daughter? And poor Tracy. How had she been able to endure this abuse by her father since she was young and not tell anyone?

This man was touted as a pillar of the community and was looked up to by so many folks, old and young. I wondered how many people knew what their revered minister was doing to his own daughter. How did Ms. Carletta not know she was married to a child molester? How can one live with another person for twenty-plus years and not realize he is a monster? Let's not talk about this God. No good God would stand by and let something like this happen to an innocent child. This former pimp-turned-child molester needed to be revealed for what he really was.

I realized that I needed to check in with Tracy. She had called several times when I was in Birmingham, but I did not have the energy or time to return the call. But, after hearing about what happened, I called her, and she picked up the phone and said, "Where have you been? I called you several times over the weekend."

"I was visiting Ty."

"You visited Ty? I didn't know you two were still an item. You haven't spoken much about him, and I have not heard rumblings from those jealous people."

"Well, there has been so much going on. Hey! Let's meet up, so we catch up."

"Sounds good. I was calling you to pick you up. My grandparents bought me a new car."

"What! What type of car did you get?"

"A drop-top 300 Series BMW!"

"Are you serious?"

"Yeah, so will 6:00 p.m. work? I'll take you out to dinner."

"I'll see you then," I said.

My heart felt heavy after hanging up with Tracy. *Are her grandparents trying to give her things as a means of reparations for the abuse she's experienced for her entire life?*

****

Tracy picked me up on time in her shiny brand-new red BMW. I had experienced a lot of "over the top" over the weekend with Ty, but Tracy was way out there. She had on makeup, was sporting a weave, wearing designer clothes, and was carrying a new Hermés bag. I can't lie; she looked like she'd walked out of one of my fashion magazines. All I really wanted to know was, *where is my girl, Trace?*

"Hey, Porchia! Meet my new girl Candy. Candy, this is my girl Porchia."

"Trace, girl, what happened to you?"

"Don't hate, biatch. You know I look good."

Did she just say bitch? I had watched many episodes of *Girlfriends,* and she sounded just like Toni Childs, one of the characters. As a matter of fact, her looks and attitude were a perfect reflection of that character.

Tracy had made reservations at Line and Lariat in Downtown Houston. We drove downtown with Tracy talking about her new life, new school, new friends, new family, all of which seemed very superficial to me.

****

When we were seated at our table in the restaurant, we started with idle chat and appetizers. I finally got tired of all the mumbo jumbo and said, "Trace, there is something I need to ask you."

"Go ahead, girl. You know that you can ask me anything."

"Is it true that your mother killed your father because he had been molesting you?"

Tracy's face dropped, and her smile disappeared. She said, "That is all in the past. I don't want to talk about it."

"Trace, you have to talk about it. You can't keep all that inside. You don't have to talk to me, but you need to talk to somebody."

"Why are you trying to upset me? I'm happy now."

"Trace, money can't buy you happiness."

"Yeah, but it can make you forget about the pain."

"Trace, I knew about the abuse because I read about it in Chanti's diary. Chanti wrote everything you said. I felt both your physical and mental pain, Tracy. That type of pain you just don't forget about. I wanted to do something but did not know how to go about it. But not once did I think that it was your father!"

I looked up and Tracy was shaking and in tears.

I grabbed her hand and said, "Trace, you don't have to go through this alone."

One of the waiters came over and asked if everything was okay. I assured him that everything was good.

"Trace, have you been seeking counseling?"

She shook her head no.

"Trace, there are resources available to help get you through this."

"My father forced me to have sex with him weekly since I was seven years old, Porchia. He called it 'our special time.' Our special time made me feel unworthy, dirty, and nasty. I feel that it was my fault. Something I must have done. Most of the time, I wish that I was never born! As I got older, he just forced himself on me. Told me he would go to my little sister if I did not cooperate. No one was there then, and no one can help me through it now!"

"He was an evil bastard, but he does not have to ruin the rest of your life, Trace. Will you let me help you?"

Chapter 19

Whoever said that life is a bitch, then you die, *lied*. Death would probably be better than a lot of the things we experience during this thing called life. I say "life is a bitch, then you are lucky when you die." Watching Mystery prepare for her wedding was a living hell on earth. Living without having my girl Chanti here with me was plain torture. However, watching Tracy go through her ordeal was like experiencing a painful death over and over.

I finally got her to agree to seek counseling. She asked me to go with her, but the psychiatrist thought it was best, under the circumstances, for her to attend alone. After about three sessions, I did notice a change and could only think that things would get better. I had school all under control, and my teammates and I had not lost a game since I went to Birmingham. I did not get a chance to miss Ty because he called me daily, and I saw him on all the ESPN highlights.

Ty made it possible that anytime that I needed to escape from the craziness of my life in Houston, I could do so. He set up a joint account with my name on it and told me it was for my travel funds. At times, I would raid my travel account to get something nice for Aunt Hattie. It was funny because she always objected but would brag to her friends about her latest gift from Baby Girl.

We took the state championship, and Keisha was named the MVP of our team and the game. I was excited because she was also graduating this year and had accepted a scholarship to Stanford. Keisha's hope was that we could take our game together to the next level. I kept what I was doing under close wraps because I was not ready to reveal my plans yet. However, when Keisha started making plans about us moving to Palo Alto, I had to tell her that I was not going to Stanford nor was I going to be playing basketball. The entire team was in shock that I had rejected my scholarship offer from Stanford and had instead accepted a full academic scholarship to Georgetown.

At the same time, my handsome, talented boyfriend was tearing up the sports world. He was invited to the NBA All-Star Weekend in Detroit, not to participate in the rookie game, but to partake in the Slam Dunk Contest. He was so excited and insisted that I be at the festivities with him. I was not certain what All-Star Weekend was supposed to be about, but my memory of it was that it was a big all-day and all-night party. The closest thing I had ever done to this was going to New Orleans during the Essence Festival and the Bayou Classic.

I'd heard a lot about Detroit being a very depressing town, but the red carpet was rolled out for the players and their families, and there was nothing but celebrations. It was great to be on Ty's arm all weekend, and I looked fabulous because I had been dressed by his personal stylist. After I'd arrived in Birmingham, Ty made certain that my hair, clothes, and nails were all done in-home. His teammates seemed to be very fond of me, although their girlfriends and wives were a little standoffish. They all seemed to be wannabe models, actresses, or singers. I did not want to bore anyone with my plans on becoming a research analyst. I did not go out of my way to engage them because frankly I had more in common with the guys, who were talking about various sports.

The most torturous night was when the guys and girls decided that they would have a night out apart. I told Ty that I would just stay at the hotel, but he pleaded with me to go out with the girls, telling me I would have fun. Unfortunately, it was quite the contrary because I spent most of my time talking to Aunt Hattie and Tracy, sharing information with them about what had happened during the weekend thus far.

"Ty, do you think I'm pretty?"

"You're beautiful, Pocahontas. Did you see how the guys were looking at you and how the girls were hating?"

"No, but I felt very awkward around the women. I don't fit in."

"You don't have to fit in with them, Pocahontas. You and I fit like a hand in a glove."

The flight attendant came by and asked flirtatiously, "Mr. Gamble, would you like a drink?"

Ty told her that he would like water.

"And what about you?"

"Yes, I would like a scotch on the rocks."

The flight attendant turned up her nose at me and walked away.

Ty looked at me and laughed. "Scotch?"

"Yes, I noticed that some of the guys were really bragging about their scotch, so I thought I would try it out. Maybe next time, I can talk to them about the best scotch."

"Ha! Sorry to disappoint you, Pocahontas, but you won't learn about the best scotch riding on a plane."

"That's okay. Unlike you, Mr. Gamble, I don't mind starting at the bottom and working my way to the top."

"Well, if that's the case, then you need to work your way to the top by joining the mile high club."

"What's the mile high club?"

"For me to know and for me to show you," he said, smirking as he led me to the bathroom.

****

When I got back to Houston, Mystery had a list of things for me to do, starting with going to get fitted for my dress. Aunt Hattie pleaded with me to be her maid of honor. I agreed but told her I was not throwing her a bridal shower. Aunt Hattie laughed and told me she would stand in for that. The Tramp's wedding to Dr. Dumb was happening in June, shortly after my graduation. I called Tracy and asked her to go with me to get fitted for Mystery's wedding.

I went to get fitted and became very upset after I saw the dress that Mystery had chosen. Tracy could not stop laughing when she saw me in it. It was a Mary Poppins dress. *Now this ho knows that she ain't Mary Poppish! She must have done this just to spite me!* I immediately called Mystery to tell her that I was not going to wear this dress.

"Porchia, I've decided to have an early 1900s-themed wedding. I coordinated your maid of honor's dress to mine. We are even going to arrive in a 1915 Ford Model T."

"Well, you're going to have to find you another maid of honor because I am not going to wear that dress."

"Porchia, please just get fitted. Perhaps we can pick a dress that is more to your liking, but they will still need your measurements."

"Bye!"

I reluctantly allowed the seamstress to take my measurements. Tracy made jokes all the way home about how I looked in that dress.

Tracy and I had planned to go out to dinner, but I convinced her to come and get a home-cooked meal at Aunt Hattie's. She could not refuse because she loved Aunt Hattie's cooking. We walked in, and there was a man talking with Aunt Hattie. He was dressed in a dark gray suit with a briefcase on his lap. Aunt Hattie looked surprised to see me. She looked at me with a very distressed face.

"Aunt Hattie, what's wrong?"

"Baby Girl, I need to speak with you in private."

"Well, Tracy was going to join us for dinner."

Aunt Hattie looked at Tracy and said, "Baby, can we make this another time?"

Tracy hugged her and said, "Sure, Aunt Hattie. I'll see you both later. Love you." Then she quickly left.

Aunt Hattie looked at the strange man and said, "Can we do this later?"

The strange man replied, "Yes. How about tomorrow?"

Aunt Hattie hesitantly agreed.

The man looked at me and, before departing, said, "It's nice to meet you, Ms. Williams."

"Baby Girl, we're going to have to have a family meeting. I already called Mystery and told her to come home as quickly as she could."

"Aunt Hattie, you're scaring me. What is it?"

"Baby Girl, I don't know where to start."

"You can start with who that man was."

"That man was an insurance man."

"So why was he here?"

"He was here to see you, Baby Girl."

"Me? Why?"

"Okay, Baby Girl, I wanted to wait until Mystery came because we both need to speak with you about this."

"Aunt Hattie, please. What's wrong?"

"That man was here to discuss the insurance disbursement that you are entitled to from your father."

"My father? I thought no one knew who my father was."

"Baby Girl, I'm so sorry."

"Aunt Hattie, please tell me."

"Your father was Pastor Charles."

My heart rate increased; I became dizzy, and my stomach was upset. I ran to the bathroom and started throwing up.

"Baby Girl! Baby Girl! Are you okay?"

I just fell on the floor and began crying uncontrollably. "Baby Girl! Open the door!"

"Just leave me be, Aunt Hattie!" I screamed.

I'm not certain how long I was in the bathroom, but I heard a gentle knocking on the door, and Mystery softly asked, "Porchia, are you okay?"

"Just leave me alone!"

"Porchia, you can't just stay locked up in there. Aunt Hattie has to use the bathroom!"

Dang! Why don't we have two bathrooms? I thought. I grabbed a towel and ran some cold water on it and wiped my face. I looked awful.

I opened the door, and Mystery was standing there with tears in her eyes. *Why is she crying?* I thought. *She doesn't care about anybody but herself.* She looked at me and responded as if she was reading my mind, "There is more that you need to hear, Porchia."

"Mystery, it can't get much worse. My father is a child-molesting, daughter-abusing monster!"

"Porchia, do you want to talk now or later?"

"What else do you all have to say? My entire life has been a lie!"

"We have a lot more to say, Porchia."

Mystery reached for my hand, and I jerked it away. She asked me to come to the kitchen, so we could all sit down and talk. Most of our family meetings had been held in the kitchen ever since I was a small child. Aunt Hattie would have baked something good and provided hot chocolate for us and coffee for herself. This meeting had nothing but the three of us around a bare table.

Mystery began talking, and Aunt Hattie was looking down, like this was going to be the worst moment in her life.

"Porchia, it is true. Pastor Charles was your father. He forced me to have sex with him when I was just a child."

"Wait! What does Pastor Charles raping *you* have to do with him being *my* father?"

"Porchia, you were born as a result of that rape."

My stomach began turning flips. *This cannot be. This tramp can't be my mother.*

"So you all lied to me and told me my mother was dead and that you were my cousin?"

Mystery responded, "Yes, I did not want you to know about the details of your birth. Aunt Hattie came to my rescue and took us both in and decided to raise

154

us both as her children. I was only eleven years old when you were born. I did not know anything about being a mother. After all, I was still a child."

I looked at Aunt Hattie and said, "I would expect that from her but not you. Why, Aunt Hattie?"

"Baby Girl, I wanted to protect you from all of that."

"But you were one of his most faithful members."

"Yes, after he came out of jail and dedicated his life to Christ, he was a different person. Or, at least, I thought he was. He apologized for everything and to everybody he had hurt. He went around trying to do good for all of the damage that he had done to people. Baby Girl, he had me convinced that he was a different person. And the Good Book teaches us to forgive as God forgives us for our transgressions. I am so sorry, Baby Girl. I only now see that he was a wolf in sheep's clothing!"

"Aunt Hattie, you said that man was here for insurance proceeds."

"Baby Girl, Pastor Charles set up a life insurance policy in the amount of $750,000 with your name on it."

I had so many more questions, but I could not stand to hear anymore, so I got up from the table and went to my room.

I went to my laptop to search for a ticket to Birmingham. I did not know whether Ty was going to be in town, but I knew that I needed to get out of here right now. I could not find a flight that departed that night, so I booked one for seven the next morning. I, then, called the limousine service that Ty used when he was in town to pick me up to take me to the airport. Mommy Liar Tramp repeatedly knocked on my door.

"Go away!"

"Porchia. I just need to know that you are okay."

"Since when? Just leave me alone!"

"Okay, but, if you want to talk, I'm here for you. I'm not going to work tonight, so I'll be here for you."

I ignored her comment. I couldn't believe that this tramp was still tricking when she was engaged to marry a doctor.

I must have cried myself to sleep because the next thing I noticed was Teddy Pendergrass crooning in my ear: *"Wake up, everybody. No more sleeping in bed."* I immediately jumped up and tiptoed to the bathroom to take a ho bath. I did not want to wake up anyone in the house, so I did not take a shower but did a wash-up from the sink.

It took me longer than I thought to get ready. Before I realized it, the driver was calling. I quickly grabbed my bags and headed out for Birmingham. I just needed to be around someone I could trust. Aunt Hattie had always been my solid rock. I thought that she was the one person I could trust with my life, but Aunt Hattie had turned out to be a liar, just like everyone else.

Chapter 20

I could not get away from this place fast enough. Once I boarded the plane, I realized I had made a mistake by booking an economy seat, instead of first class. This big man was sitting in the middle of me and another lady. He had a tendency to lean to my side when he fell asleep. He was reeking of cheap cologne and liquor. My stomach turned the entire flight. When the plane landed, I immediately ran to the bathroom to throw up.

I decided not to call Ty's driver to take me to his place. Instead, I took a taxi to surprise him. The drive seemed like an eternity. I badly desired a hot bubble bath and Ty's strong arms holding me. He was the only person left that I could trust. I didn't know what I would do if he was not a part of my life.

I was not certain whether Ty was on the road or not, but it didn't matter. I would be there when he arrived. I opened to door to find the house quiet. I first went to the kitchen to grab some water. Ty's housekeeper had not made it yet because there were leftover dishes in the sink. I quickly downed the water because a bath, and hopefully strong arms, kisses, and more were waiting for me upstairs.

I could hear noise coming from Ty's room, so I was happy to know that he was home. As I opened the door, I said, "Surprise, baby!"

There was Ty, in a doggy-style position, with the shooting guard, Raheem, for the Slammers, pumping Ty like he was going for the shot of his life. I must have stood there for a few seconds because Ty jumped out of bed. While reaching for his shorts on the floor, he stumbled and said, "Wait! Pocahontas, I can explain."

I ran out of the house and down the street. After that, everything went black.

Chapter 21

I don't understand. That looks like me. Where am I? Why is everybody standing over me crying? Mystery is here and is completely losing it.

"Mystery! Mystery! I'm right here. Can't you see me?"

Oh no! Aunt Hattie just ran out of the room, all 350 pounds of her flailing, and yelling, "Oh, Jesus! Oh, Jesus!"

Let me go get Aunt Hattie.

"Aunt Hattie, what's up?" *Dang! She is fast for a big woman.* "Aunt Hattie!"

Maybe Mystery can tell me what's going on. Let me go back to the room.

Mystery, between her tears, asked, "Doctor, do you think she will wake up soon?"

"She still has a lot of swelling around her brain, but we are remaining positive, and I ask that you do, too."

So I've lost consciousness, and I'm in the hospital. It all came rushing back to me like a flash of lightning. *Oh, hell yeah. I caught Ty with his teammate having sex. I ran from the house. I must have been in an accident when I ran from the house. Now I'm lying in a state of unconsciousness. As I said, "life is a bitch, and you are lucky if you die." My best friend is dead. My father was a pimp, a child-abusing, incestuous rapist molester. The person I trusted the most in the world has lied to me for my whole entire life, and the guy I trusted and fell in love with likes guys.*

Why am I still here? I wondered. The moment I asked that question a bright light appeared. I was drawn to this beautiful bright light. I felt a warm, loving presence. More love than I had ever felt during my lifetime. I thought Aunt Hattie had given me warmth, love, and safety, but this was a lot stronger.

A voice that could not be identified as male or female said, "Hello, my child."

"Who are you?

"I Am," said the Light.

"You are who?" I asked.

"The Alpha and the Omega."

"I see you like to talk in riddles."

"You should listen to me with your heart, not your ears."

"I have tried listening with my heart, but that does not work."

"You have experienced a lot during your lifetime, but your time on this earth is not over. You still have a lot to accomplish."

"I don't want to experience this life anymore. I have nothing more to live for."

"My child, your time is not yet done. I can't tell you that there will be no more heartache, but you will have me with you."

"Why are you here?"

"You said one time, if there is a God, that I needed to reveal myself to you. So here I am."

"God?"

"Yes, I am He."

"Bullshit! If you do exist, why is there so much cruelty in this world?"

"My child, I did not create the cruelty. When I created Adam and Eve, it was in purity and without sin. Once Adam and Eve entered the Garden of Eden and ate of the forbidden fruit of knowledge, good and evil then came into existence. From that point on, men were born into sin. But through me, men can be delivered from sin. But it is a choice that one must make."

The more the voice spoke to me, feelings of love and security embraced my entire being. I felt complete peace and knew that anything and everything was possible.

"God, what am I to do?"

"You are to go back and embrace all of the things I represent: love, forgiveness, hope, joy, peace, kindness, compassion, goodness, and patience. For you to get through the trials and tribulations that you will face, you will need to have complete faith in me. Know that I am with you through both the good and bad times. Faith can only be demonstrated by your actions. Listen to me with your heart, my child, and you will succeed through your earthly journey."

I was crying because I knew that, in the past, I had doubted Him, cursed Him, and told others He did not exist.

"Lord, I am so sorry. How do I ensure that I meet you again?"

"You accept Jesus, who came to this earth so that you would not perish, as your personal Savior. This way, we will meet again, and you will enjoy the benefits of the life you were promised before Adam and Eve ate of the forbidden fruit."

The Light then said, "It is time for you to continue your journey, my child. Remember, I am with you."

The Light began moving away, and I felt a warmth go inside of me as I returned to the still body lying on the hospital bed.

"Porchia, baby, can you hear me?" I could hear Mystery's voice. I opened my eyes and Mystery shouted, "Aunt Hattie, she's up!"

Aunt Hattie ran over and said, "Baby Girl! Baby Girl, you are back! God answers prayers."

I just smiled at both of them. I wished I could get up and hug them. Aunt Hattie told Mystery to go get the nurse and let her know.

Within minutes, the doctor was in my room.

"Well, hello, there, missy. It's nice to see you."

"Nice to be here," I mumbled.

I struggled to read his name tag. "How long have I been here?"

"You have been here for four days."

Out of the corner of my eye, I saw a man holding Aunt Hattie. It must have been Dr. Little. I thought, *That's nice of him to be here for Mystery.*

162

The doctor looked back and asked, "Can I have a moment to check out Porchia?"

"No problem. Baby Girl, we'll be right outside," said Aunt Hattie.

I muttered, "Thanks, Aunt Hattie."

The doctor looked into my eyes and asked me to move my eyes in different directions, felt around my head, listened to my heartbeat, then took my blood pressure. He took a seat next to me and told me that he would have to run some additional tests, including an MRI today, but it looked like I was healing pretty well.

"Doctor, I feel like I was hit by a truck."

"Well, young lady, you *were* hit by a truck. Luckily, it was not that big or moving that fast. You don't have any breaks, just a lot of swelling and bruising." He hesitated before saying, "But I am sorry that you lost the baby."

Tears began forming in my eyes.

I was pregnant? Then I thought about it. Ty and I always had protected sex. The condom had come off once, but Ty said it was intact. If I had gotten pregnant, I also needed to find out if I'd caught any diseases.

"Doc, can you test me for sexually transmitted diseases, including HIV?"

"Yes, we have done that already, and everything came back negative."

That was a big relief!

After the doc finished his examination, Aunt Hattie, Mystery, and Ty came into the room. My heart began beating fast when I saw Ty. *Oh my God! The man I saw was Ty. I don't think I can face him right now. God, you promised that you would be here for me, and I need you now.*

Aunt Hattie and Mystery came close while Ty hung back. They kissed me and told me they were glad I was okay.

Aunt Hattie said, "Well, Baby Girl, we're going to give you some time alone with Ty."

I wanted to say "no," but my tongue was frozen. When they left the room, Ty approached the bed. His face was sunken, and his eyes were red.

"I'm so sorry, Pocahontas. I did not mean for any of this to happen. And you must believe me when I say I love you. These have been the worst four days of my life."

Okay, God, you said you would be with me, and all I want to do is cuss this man out. I want to tell him that I see he likes playing tight end, so he needs to take his now not-so-tight-end somewhere to get fucked. Yes, that was what I wanted to say. Instead, I said, "Ty, can we talk about this later? I'm not up to having a conversation about this yet."

"Sure, you can have all the time you need."

Did this muthafuka just give me permission to be upset?

"Thanks. I appreciate that. I'll call you when I'm ready to talk."

"Are you asking me to leave?"

"Yes, please."

"But—"

I interrupted him and said, "Ty, we'll talk later."

When he kissed me on my forehead, I cringed. He walked toward the door and before leaving, said, "I do love you, Pocahontas."

God, I know that my thoughts count, not just my words, so please work on me! Work on my heart, mind, and thoughts.

Aunt Hattie and Mystery walked into the room. I looked at Mystery and asked if I could speak with Aunt Hattie alone. Mystery looked a little disappointed but was cooperative.

"Baby Girl, I'm sorry for everything. You were right. I should have been honest with you."

"Aunt Hattie, hush. I want to tell you something. I know that you love me and that you were only doing what you thought was right at that time. You have attempted to protect me and provide me guidance my entire life. I forgive you."

Aunt Hattie looked at me with tears in her eyes and said, "Baby, you might forgive me, but I'm having a difficult time forgiving myself. Despite everything, you have turned out to be a lovely young woman."

"Aunt Hattie, you had a lot to do with the way I turned out. And I love you."

"I love you, too, Baby Girl." Aunt Hattie gave me a big hug.

"Ouch, Aunt Hattie, that hurts."

Aunt Hattie laughed and said, "I'm sorry, Baby Girl."

"I'm good. Aunt Hattie. I need to speak with Mystery alone now. Do you mind getting her?"

"Anything for you, Baby Girl."

Mystery walked in hesitantly, looking at me nervously, and asked, "Porchia, are you okay?"

"Mystery, before we start talking, I have one very important question for you."

"Yes?"

"Why in the hell did you name me Porchia?"

"I liked the car."

"Well, did you know it's pronounced differently and spelled P-O-R-S-C-H-E?"

"Really?"

I had to laugh. *My poor mother. Did I actually just think about Mystery as my mother in my thoughts? Ugh.*

"Porchia, I'm so sorry. I never thought I could be a good role model for you. That's why I was okay when Aunt Hattie said she would raise you as her own. I was only a child myself. I went along with the story that your mom had died for lack of a better one. I tried to do what I thought was best at the time. I grew up with a mother who was a drug-addicted prostitute. She died from an overdose. Her mother ran a whorehouse and pimped her to men at an early age. My grandmother, as the story was told, was killed by a john who said she had robbed him. I don't have good genes or a good upbringing. I called it the DuBois curse. And I had to do everything in my power to protect you from it."

"Mystery, breathe. I want to apologize to you."

"Apologize to me?" she said, surprised.

"Yes, I apologize for the way I have treated you my entire life. I apologize for calling you out of your name almost every day. I apologize for treating you as if your life did not matter. I apologize for not thanking you for the financial support."

Mystery placed her finger on my lips, then took my hand in hers, and simply said, "I have always loved you and will always love you."

It felt great to know the truth about who I was. But I would not allow my biological makeup to define me.

Can't Nobody

Chapter 22

I had been dealing with a lot that I had not spoken to anyone about. I missed Chanti so much. She would have been my sounding board for everything that was going on. I'd lost a baby that I did not know I was carrying. I had not spoken with Ty, despite the fact that he had been blowing up my phone for days. I knew I should be forgiving, but my heart was not there yet.

I was still trying to cope with the fact that Mystery was my biological mother. And not to mention the fact that I had three sisters and two brothers. I had been avoiding my sister, Tracy, because I was not certain what I was supposed to say to her. Believe me, I had been having a lot of conversations with God. It seemed like He was busy because I had not gotten a lot of answers.

After information was leaked to the press about my father and his abuse of Tracy, several young girls came forward, saying that they had also been abused by the good ole Pastor Charles. I thought death had been too easy for him. He should have had to face some type of lifetime torture for all the pain he had caused everyone.

I had been reading the Bible, and I was very familiar with the scripture where God says vengeance is His. But I was not certain what type of punishment was fitting for a man pretending that he was one of God's chosen men. I believed that so many people were able to be easily misled by so-called Men of God because we didn't have enough understanding of His Word and because we put too much faith in men, instead of in God.

My phone rang, and it was Tracy again. I guess I couldn't avoid her forever.

"Hello."

"Hey, Porchia. I've been calling you for days. How are you? I heard you were in an accident. What happened?"

I immediately thought that this was a bad idea because I did not want to rehash everything that had happened.

"I was hit by a truck."

"Girl, how did you get hit by a truck? You were in Alabama, right?"

"Yes, visiting Ty. I don't want to talk about me. How are you doing?"

"Well, the counseling is helping me a lot. But since the media heard about what he did, it's been a zoo around here. We can't leave the house without reporters following us. I feel so embarrassed that the world knows what he did to me!"

"Trace, it is not your fault. He was a sick man!"

"Still, it doesn't make me feel better."

"I know, Trace. But I'm here for you. We need to get together really soon."

"Okay, I love you, Porchia."

"I love you, too, sis."

Can't Nobody

Oh no, did I just say that? I don't think she understood what I just said.

"See you soon," Tracy said.

I was glad that she did not have any idea that we are sisters.

****

I was going back to school but really was not feeling anything. I got through the day. Mr. Papal tried to convince me that I was still on track and I could still go through with my plans. I had a lot of mail from different universities but had ignored it all. Mr. Papal told me that Georgetown was trying to get in touch to see if my plans were the same.

I guess I was supposed to be going to some type of orientation soon. This was really all too much for me to process. I had no energy to do anything. Many days, I just wished that God would have let me just go on. I was not certain what type of plans He had for me, but this was the toughest period of my life. And I did not have anyone here to help me through this period. I went back to what Aunt Hattie always said—"Nobody can do me like Jesus." I attempted to stay in close contact with Him, hoping that He would reveal His master plan real soon.

I came home from school ready to relax, and there was Ty, sitting with Aunt Hattie, turning on his charm. I was too embarrassed to tell anyone about why I had run out of Ty's house.

"Well, hi, Baby Girl. Look who's here to see you. I'm going to let you two visit."

"Aunt Hattie, you are looking wonderful as usual," said Ty.

"Thank you, baby." Aunt Hattie left the room, and I just stood looking at him.

"Pocahontas, we need to talk."

"My name is Porchia."

"We need to talk, Porchia."

I snapped, "Talk then!"

"Not here. Can we go somewhere to have a little privacy?"

"I feel more comfortable here."

Before Ty could say anything, Mystery came running into the house in tears. She bypassed us like we were not even there and went to her room. Mystery could be a little dramatic, so I did not know what was going on, but she was crying so loudly that Aunt Hattie ran out of her room and knocked on her door.

"Ty, seems like we're having a family emergency. We'll have to finish this later."

"Okay, Pocahontas. I need to fly out tonight, but hopefully we can talk before I leave."

I walked over to the door, opened it, and said, "Bye, Ty."

He slowly walked out the door, looked back, and said, "I won't give up on us."

I hurried to Mystery's room, and she was still bawling while Aunt Hattie was trying to comfort her.

I sat down next to her and asked, "What's wrong?"

Sniffling and breathing hard, she said, "He called off our wedding. He said I was a spoiled woman since I'd already had a child."

"What?" I asked.

Mystery screamed, "He said he wanted a woman that has not had any children. His wife would have only *his* children."

In my mind, I was like, *He was willing to marry a stripper as long as she had no evidence of children? This man is really a joke!*

"Mystery, he's a jerk who is living in the medieval times! You don't need anyone like that. You deserve better."

"I don't deserve better. I have not been a good person."

"Mystery, that is nonsense. You are a very generous and loving." *Perhaps with too many,* I thought. Then, I continued, "You're a woman who deserves to be treated like a queen by a man who loves her as much as she loves him."

I was not certain where all of those words had come from.

Aunt Hattie said, "Listen to her, baby. She's very wise for her age. You know we have always said that Baby Girl has been here before."

I had to smile at Aunt Hattie speaking as if I was not there.

"Come on, Mystery. Get cleaned up, and you, me, and Aunt Hattie will go out on the town. Dress to impress, both of you."

****

Aunt Hattie walked out with a sequined dress that I did not know she even had with a matching handbag and shoes.

"Baby Girl, how are you taking us out on a night on the town?"

"I have a little rainy day fund compliments of Mr. Tyrese Gamble."

I checked my account earlier, and I had a balance of over $35,000 in my account. My first thought was to tell him to withdraw the money and close the account, but, on second thought, I figured it was only a small amount for the pain and suffering I had experienced because of his actions.

Mystery came out of the room looking like she was on her way to the Academy Awards. She was wearing a Jovani evening dress with all of the coordinating accessories, including the shoes and a bag. She could have competed with any of the women who walked the red carpet.

I never noticed that she was so stunning. She announced that this outfit was for a function that she was supposed to attend with Dr. Fake. He told her to spare no expense and gave her his platinum American Express card.

"Girl, those shoes are bad," I said.

"Yeah, they're Jimmy Choos."

"Jimmy whose?" exclaimed Aunt Hattie with a perplexed look on her face.

Mystery and I just laughed. Then we all hugged and walked out of door.

Can't Nobody

Chapter 23

"Lord, give me the strength to make it through this day that you have made. Your glory is astounding, and your mercy is enduring. You have met me and led me to a place that I never thought I would be. I have endured trials and tribulations that I could not otherwise have handled without your presence and Word leading me. Lord, please let me be able to meet Ty and get the closure that we both need to go forth with our journey. Lord, I also pray that you are with me as I speak with Tracy. Lord, you are the Master of all things, and I know that all things work for the good for those who believe in you. Amen."

A week had passed, and I had not spoken to Ty, so we made arrangements to speak. We met at the park where we first met. I found a bench where there was complete privacy. He walked up and sat down. All I could think was, *Dang! This man is fine.* I started thinking about the baby we'd lost and what our life would have been like if I had not caught him.

"Hello, Porchia. Thanks for agreeing to meet with me. This place brings back a lot of memories. This place is where I laid eyes on the woman I wanted to be my wife."

Wow! He called me Porchia, I thought.

"Ty, how could you say that?"

"I have loved you since the first day I laid eyes on you."

"Ty, stop. This won't get us anywhere. After all, you like men."

"Pocahontas, it's not that black and white."

"Do you like men? Yes or no?"

"Pocahontas, for the first time in my life, I found someone that I loved unconditionally. Someone that I would like to spend the rest of my life with. Someone I would like to have my babies." He paused. "Yes, I think about the baby and mourn our loss every day."

"Ty, how can you say all of that? The baby was a mistake."

"God makes no mistakes."

I did not say anything, but I agreed with him totally on that point. God makes no mistakes, and that was why there was no baby.

"Ty, how are we supposed to live happily ever after? You like men."

Ty took a deep breath. "I have never spoken to anyone about this. My mom was impregnated by a man at age fifteen. She later found out that he was married. He vanished from her life once he found out that she was pregnant. My mom ended up dropping out of school, so she could take care of me, her baby. Her family helped us as much as they could, but they also were struggling. I wore hand-me-downs until third grade. I was the center of every conceivable 'your momma so poor' joke that you could think of. I was nine years old when my mom met a man who changed our lives forever. He made certain we were financially provided for, and, in return, he sexually abused me. At first, it was him playing with my penis. Then, he would have me play with his penis. He would give me money in return for these acts. When I got older, I knew what he was doing was wrong, and I would refuse. But that was when he would force himself on me."

"What?"

"Yes, this lasted from age nine to thirteen until he was busted for stealing drugs from where he worked and selling them on the streets."

"Did you tell your mother?"

"No, I did not tell anyone."

"Why did you not tell anyone?"

"I didn't know who to tell, and if I did, I didn't think anyone would believe me. He not only took care of us, but took care of my extended family. Everyone loved him."

"But, Ty . . ."

Ty had tears running down his face. "Let me finish, Pocahontas. So I just endured the abuse. I was a withdrawn child most of my life. I did not have many friends. I started going out to play basketball as a means to escape and forget about the abuse. I started spending more time on the court than I spent at home. By the time I started high school, I put everything I had into basketball and excelled at it. At an early age, I decided that I would go to college to become a psychiatrist, so I could help children like myself who were sexually abused. Although I never had a relationship with anyone during high school, girls chased me all the time. I met a football player in high school, and we became good friends. He was one of the most popular guys on the team, and he dated the captain of the cheerleading team. One night, I was at his house, and he came on to me. I actually enjoyed it. It was not like the sex that happened when I was a kid. It actually felt good."

"Ty, this is too much."

"Let me finish, Pocahontas, please," Ty pleaded.

I felt in my spirit that I should be there to listen to him.

"Well, we carried on our sexual relationship up until the time he graduated and went away to college in the state of Washington. He was a year ahead of me. No one knew about this sexual relationship but us."

"So you never had a girlfriend in high school?"

"No, I just had friends, and people assumed that I was having sex with them. I was never really attracted to girls. But at the same time, I was not attracted to guys. The sex was just a physically gratifying act for me."

"Have you ever had sex with a woman?"

"Yes, once I went to college, and although it was satisfying, it was not as satisfying as the sex I had with my guy friend."

I got up and walked away, not really wanting to hear more. Ty followed me and started talking again.

"But that all changed when I met you. I want to get to know every part of you, your mind, heart, body, and soul. I connect with you in a manner I have never connected with another person. I want to be there for you in any way that I can. Having sex with you is over the top. I feel that our bodies are one, and that every time is the first time. I know that you are the one I want to spend the rest of my life with. When you showed up that night, I actually had called Raheem over to break off our relationship."

"Does his wife know about the two of you?"

"No, she has no idea."

"So why were you having sex with him?"

"As I said, I called him over, so I could break it off, and it just happened."

"So it just happened that your clothes came off, his clothes came off, and then there he was penetrating you!"

"Pocahontas, I can't explain it. But I knew that was the last time I would be with him."

"How could you say that, Ty? I'm not a man, and I don't have a penis. What are you gonna do if you get that craving again?"

"I don't know. All I know is that I want to spend the rest of my life with you."

"Ty, I can't do it. You may not think that you are gay, but men don't just sleep with other men."

I looked at him, and he looked as if he had lost his only friend in the world.

"Ty, I still love you, but I will have to love you from a distance. You will be in my prayers."

"Pocahontas, please don't give up on me."

"I'm not. I am leaving you in the hands of the Lord."

After my meeting with Ty, I was somewhat relieved but knew that was only one tough conversation completed. Tracy called me before I could call her and asked me to go bowling. I knew that I had to take this opportunity to have a conversation with her. I was not looking forward to it because I was not certain how she would take the news with all that she had been through. We made arrangements to meet the following day.

****

I saw Tracy from a distance, as she came running and smiling and said, "Porchia, why did you not tell me that you and I were sisters? This is great! I'm so excited. You are not only my girl, but you are my girl sister. I love it," Tracy said, while jumping up and down and squeezing me.

I was totally in shock and was not certain how to respond. "Trace, how did you find out?"

"I told my grandmother I was coming to meet you, and she said it was great. And that she was glad that, as sisters, we were close. I did not understand until she went on to explain that your mom and my dad had had a sexual relationship."

"Well, Trace, I'm not certain it was consensual since she was only a child, but, yes, there was sex, and I am here as a result of it."

"Anyway, girl, I'm just glad that we're related!"
God, thank you!

Tracy then grabbed me and said, "C'mon, sister! Let's get a game going!"

We had a good time, but something bothered me about her reaction. She seemed to be repressing the things that our pervert father had done to her, Mystery, and the other young girls. Tracy just insisted that the counseling was helping her deal with all of her issues. *Perhaps I should go to counseling as well because I'm not coping as well as she demonstrates that she is*, I thought. I was not certain how to approach Tracy . . . as a friend or a sister.

Perhaps just treating her as I always had would be enough. I didn't understand the sister role and wanted to ensure that I was doing what was necessary to be supportive. I also wanted a relationship with my younger siblings. I was really uncertain on how to go about that. I had a lot of unanswered questions about many of the things that were happening in my life, including my relationship with Mystery. And even more difficult was, how was I ever going to get over the feelings that I had for Ty? By the time we departed from the park, we both had tears in our eyes. Ty embraced me, and he cried loudly. I felt the same way I'd felt the first time he touched me. My whole body quivered. There was no denying it; I was still in love with Ty.

Can't Nobody

Chapter 24

I could not believe I was on a plane headed to D.C. to attend an orientation for recipients of the Research Scholarship at Georgetown University against my better judgment. After much discussion with Principal Ashton and Mr. Papal, they convinced me that I should not pass up on this opportunity of a lifetime. However, my life and situation had completely changed since I initially accepted Georgetown's offer. I felt that I needed to be closer to home for Aunt Hattie, Mystery, and my new sisters and brothers. Although Aunt Hattie seemed to be doing well, she had not completely recovered. She was also seeing a new doctor since Dr. Fake had broken off his engagement with Mystery. This new doctor did not seem to be as competent or compassionate toward here as Dr. Fake. He had prescribed Aunt Hattie a drug that she was allergic to. Luckily, the pharmacist caught the error.

I had been thinking a lot lately about Mystery bearing all of the burden of taking care of Aunt Hattie. She was right; she had a life to live also, and this was unfair to her. With the insurance proceeds that I received from the incestuous, molesting, child-abusing former pimp pastor, I could help out financially. If I left, Aunt Hattie would be spending her nights alone. Mystery tried to convince me that she could find a day job, but she had limited skills. I was not certain how dancing and stripping would transfer to a well-paying day job. She had some half-baked idea about seeking finances to open a gentleman's restaurant/bar that catered to lunch professionals.

I arrived at National, and there was a tall, handsome Italian man, standing there, holding a sign with my name written on it. This made me think about my first trip to Alabama, where Ty had had the driver carry a giant sign with "Pocahontas" written on it.

"Hello. Are you Ms. Porchia?" asked the man, carrying the sign.

"Yes, sir. It's me in the flesh."

"There's another person arriving from Chicago in five minutes. I hope you are okay with waiting."

"Are you giving me a choice?" I asked teasingly.

He looked at me without smiling and responded, "Yes, you do. You could always take a taxi to the university."

Whoa! I wondered who had ruffled his feathers today.

"I suppose I can wait another five minutes, but a minute more will be unacceptable."

The handsome sign man seemed to crack a slight smile.

"Hi, Pocahontas, what are you doing here?"

I looked up, and it was Ty's lover's wife.

"Hey, Jinn. Why are you here?"

"I'll be attending Georgetown and working under Professor Piaget," she responded.

"Me, too, but I thought we were waiting for someone from Chicago."

"The Slammers played the Bulls, and I just came from Chicago, instead of Alabama."

"Wow! This is a surprise. I thought you were like the rest of them—an actress, model, or singer."

"I guess we both made assumptions. I thought your only love, besides Ty, was basketball."

"Ladies, I apologize for interrupting the reunion, but I would like to introduce myself. I am Professor Piaget, and I am delighted to meet you both. So, Ms. Porchia, do you prefer to be called Pocahontas?"

I wanted to run back to Houston. I had never felt this embarrassed before. Not because of the Pocahontas comment, but because I had been so flippant when I first met him.

"No, Professor Piaget, Porchia will do just fine. And I apologize for my previous comments."

"No problem," he said smiling. "I found them to be quite entertaining."

We drove through the District, and I saw many sights that I hoped I would have time to visit before I left. Jinn was just chatting away. I didn't realize that she was this chatty when we were in Detroit. As a matter of fact, I didn't recall her saying much. I wondered, *Does she know her husband sleeps with men?*

"Pocahontas, did you hear me?"

"No, I am sorry, Jinn. My mind was elsewhere. But can I ask you a favor? Could you call me Porchia?"

"Oh, I didn't realize you didn't like Pocahontas because when Ty speaks of you, he always calls you Pocahontas."

"Yeah, I know. That's Ty's personal way of taunting me."

"Well, Porchia it is. So when was the last time you saw Ty?"

I wanted to say shortly after I found him in bed with your husband but answered, "About two weeks ago."

If this girl does not stop asking me questions about Ty, she will find out something she doesn't want to know, I thought. I was so happy when we pulled up to the campus, mainly because Jinn's chattering ceased. I was impressed by the beauty of the campus and the historic buildings. I had never seen anything like this, not even in New Orleans. As Professor Piaget was showing us around, I thought that I could easily fit in here. I would be a long way from Houston, but perhaps it would be a welcomed change.

Professor Piaget, after our tour of the campus, told us that we had time to freshen up before going to the lab. He escorted us to our dormitory where we would be staying for the week. To my disappointment, Jinn and I were sharing a room. I was not certain I would be able to get through the week with her. Professor Piaget told us that he would have a student pick us up and escort us to the lab in about an hour.

Once he departed, Jinn looked at me and said, "Dayuuum, he is fine! He looks too young to be a professor. I wonder how old is he? So, Porchia, which bed do you want?"

Dang! Does she breathe between sentences? "It doesn't matter, either one."

"Okay, I'll take this one."

She chose the bed closest to the bathroom, and I was left with the bed near the window which was the one I preferred anyway.

"Well, I need to call my doting husband. He's probably going out of his mind with worry."

I rolled my eyes and thought, *If you only knew.*

"Hi, honey! Guess who's here with me? Guess!" Pause. "Pocahontas!"

Did I not just ask her to not call me Pocahontas? This girl is gonna make me lose my newfound religion.

"So Ty didn't tell you that she was coming here? You all seem to be so close."

Yeah. If only you knew how close. I started unpacking, pretending I was not listening to her phone call. I bet Mr. Raheem was shaking at the news that we were roommates.

"Porchia, Raheem was really surprised that we were roommates."

Yeah, surprised is probably an understatement.

"Understandably so, because Ty doesn't know."

"What? Your honey doesn't know that you're spending a week at Georgetown?"

"Jinn, you have not given me a chance to tell you that Ty and I are taking a break. There are a lot of things that I need to figure out."

"What! Are you okay?"

"No, it's been difficult, but, with God on my side, I'll make it." I smiled hearing Aunt Hattie's voice proclaiming that "nobody can do me like Jesus."

"Well, I'm certain you two will work it out soon. You're like Jack and Jill."

Did she just say Jack and Jill? "Time will tell was the only thing I could think about saying.

"Well, I'm going to take a shower and change out of these clothes. Do you need to use the bathroom?" she asked.

"No, I'm good." I was so glad when she went into the bathroom. I didn't know how I was going to make it through the weekend with Chatterbox.

The student chaperone could not show up fast enough for me. When he did, he escorted us around campus, showing us things from a student's perspective before going to the lab. Professor Piaget was already in the lab, working and looking even more handsome in his white lab coat. He showed us different areas of the lab and introduced us to the project that we would be working on together.

After our introduction to our project, we had to go to an evening reception with other prospective students in other areas of the research department. I worked the room to avoid Jinn and ended up meeting people from all over the States and a few foreign countries. There was one guy from India that I found particularly interesting. He surprised me because he was sporting the European hip-hop look with the saggy skinny jeans, a T-shirt, and a tight blazer. The turban on his head completed the look. He explained to me that he was not Hindu. He was Sikh. He was well versed in American politics, music, sports, and culture.

I decided to go to dinner with my new Indian friend, Ravinder, who I found out preferred to be called Ravi. Ravi was like a breath of fresh air. He didn't talk much but seemed to have interesting tidbits to share. I don't know how we started talking about orgasms, but he said that a pig's orgasm lasts thirty minutes, only second to a camel's. I started wondering if he had a thing for animals or something. But he seemed to be one that just liked to recite interesting facts, like the human body carries about three to five pounds of bacteria. I immediately felt the need to do a cleansing.

Ravi did ask questions about me and my family. He seemed impressed that I was an inner-city child, who grew up in the hood. Ravi explained that he grew up in the region of Punjab, India, where his father was a steel mill owner. They lived quite comfortably with a nanny, housekeeper, and driver who were all treated as family because they did not believe in the caste system. Everyone should be treated fairly and not based on socioeconomic conditions.

The remainder of the week at Georgetown passed by extremely fast. I avoided Chatterbox, not only because she talked too much, but also because I did not want to be the one to fill her in on the fact that her man was a switch hitter. Usually, by the time I returned to the room, she was fast asleep.

Ravi and I spent most of our days and nights together. We toured D.C. and even rode something called a "Hop-On Hop-Off" bus where we toured the city and stopped at places of interest like the monuments, the cemetery, and the White House.

I thought we were hanging out as friends, having a good time . . . until Ravi attempted to kiss me one night after walking me to my room. I had to let him know that I really enjoyed kicking it with him, but did not like him that way. I could see that he was really hurt, but he seemed to take it well because we enjoyed each other's company after the missed kiss.

As soon as I left Georgetown, I couldn't wait to return. I couldn't help but anticipate the start of my first semester of college. I still worried about Aunt Hattie, Mystery, Tracy, and making a connection with my other siblings, but, with God on my side, I knew that anything could be accomplished. I felt more confident these days than I had ever felt prior to meeting Him. I knew that He would be the conductor of my life. I was committed to listening to Him with my heart and doing as He instructed me.

Chapter 25

I walked in, and Aunt Hattie was walking around dusting and singing, "Jesus is on the main line. Tell Him what you want. Oooh, Jesus is on the main line. Tell Him what you want."

I interrupted her singing. "If you want your aunt to rest, tell Him what you want. I would like my aunt to rest. Tell Him what you want. I am telling Him what I want right now."

Aunt Hattie ran and hugged me and said, "Oh, Baby Girl, I'm so happy that you're home. I missed you so much."

"I missed you, too, Aunt Hattie. But what are you doing?"

"Baby Girl, I can't just sit around here. And I'm feeling much better than I have felt in years."

"You do look good, Aunt Hattie. You done lost a few pounds, too."

"Yes, five pounds to be exact. I'll be back to my high school weight soon, and when I am, y'all better watch out."

I laughed and said, "Slow your roll, Al Sharpton."

Aunt Hattie slapped me on my butt and said, "You ain't too old for me to beat you, girl."

"You're going to have to catch me first," I said, running to my room.

I put down my bags and went back to Aunt Hattie. "So how's Mystery? Has she gotten over Dr. Dumb?"

Aunt Hattie laughed loudly. "Baby Girl, you have a name for everybody, don't you?

Have you made up with that nice young man?"

"No, Aunt Hattie, I don't think I will."

"Baby Girl, let's go to the kitchen. I'd like to talk to you about a few things."

We walked hand-in-hand to the kitchen. As Aunt Hattie started making coffee, I thought, *Oh no! This must be a serious.*

"Aunt Hattie, what's on your mind?"

"Baby Girl, I've noticed that there's been a change in you. You've been caring and supportive of Mystery. You are not as high-strung as you normally are."

Wow! She thinks I'm high-strung.

"You seem to have a new presence about yourself. But why are you not speaking to that nice young man anymore? You don't have that same sparkle in your eye like when he was around."

"Aunt Hattie, there's a lot that I have not said."

Aunt Hattie brought the cups to the table and sat down. "Well, are you ready to talk about it?"

"This is just as good a time as any, I guess. You know, Aunt Hattie, it's sort of weird. I know that Mystery is my mother, but I still can't open up to her."

"That's okay, Baby Girl. It'll take time."

"But what if it never happens? What if I never develop a mother-daughter bond with her?"

"Porchia, you can't force anything. And you may never have that bond that you're looking for. But you still can have a healthy, good, loving relationship with Mystery. But, Baby Girl, I think you're just putting off what we need to talk about."

"Well, I haven't spoken about the accident."

"No, you have not."

"Well, the reason I got into an accident in the first place was because I was running away from Ty's house."

"Baby Girl, you ran away from here to go to Ty. Then, you ran away from Ty. Why you doing all that running, Baby Girl?"

"Aunt Hattie, when I walked in Ty's house, I caught him in bed—"

Aunt Hattie interrupted me, "You mean that nice young man was cheating on you with another woman?"

"Yes, he was cheating but not with a woman."

Aunt Hattie gasped and said, "Baby, are you telling me Ty has some sugar in his tank?"

I laughed, "Aunt Hattie, he had more than sugar in his tank."

"All right, Baby Girl, I don't need to hear no details."

"Well, I was running away from his house after I caught him and his teammate together."

"It was another man that played basketball with him?"

"Yes, Aunt Hattie. But what I also discovered was that I was pregnant when I had the accident."

"Baby Girl, hush!"

"Aunt Hattie, please don't tell Mystery. This is a conversation between you and me."

"Now you know I would never do that! I'm very saddened that you've been going through this all alone."

"But, Aunt Hattie, the good news is that I have not been going through this alone."

"What do you mean?"

"When I was unconscious, I met God. I did not see Him. He came to me as a Bright Light. That Bright Light had a heart-to-heart conversation with me."

Aunt Hattie surprised me and started crying.

"Aunt Hattie, what's wrong? This is good news."

She responded by getting up and doing a dance, chanting, "All praises go up to you. Thank you, Lord. My prayers have been answered. Thank you, Almighty. Thank you, Lord."

Aunt Hattie must have carried on with her praise worship for about five minutes. I was worried about her heart, so I got up and hugged her just so she would stop.

Mystery walked in when we were embracing.

"Welcome home, Porchia! What's going on?"

I said, "We're just celebrating God's goodness. God is good all the time."

Aunt Hattie responded with, "All the time, God is good."

I grabbed Mystery, and we all three hugged silently for a while. If there was ever a Kodak moment with our crew, this would definitely be it. Six months ago, if someone told me I would be hugging Mystery and have feelings of love for her, I would have called that person everything but a child of God and perhaps had a few choice words for God because, if He existed, He was public enemy number one as far as I was concerned. It felt good to know that I had come so far, and it felt even better to know that He was not through with me yet.

Can't Nobody

Chapter 26

Ravi called me a couple of times, and we spoke about how excited we were to be going to Georgetown and graduation. I was surprised that I also heard from Chatterbox. She was reaching out to find out if I would be her roommate during the year. I could not find an excuse to say no, so I agreed to do it. She also inquired about the status of my and Ty's relationship, and I just pretty much told her it was on ice. Ty had actually left me a couple of messages, sent gifts to the house, and attempted one visit where I refused to see him. I attempted to make it clear to him I would see him and talk to him on my terms.

The last communication from Ty was an e-mail that read: "HI, POCAHONTAS. I HOPE THIS E-MAIL FINDS YOU DOING WELL. I HAVE BEEN SEEKING COUNSELING AND HAVE LEARNED A LOT ABOUT MYSELF. ONE THING I HAD TO DO WAS WRITE A LETTER TO MY ABUSER AND TELL HIM THAT I FORGAVE HIM. COUNSELING HAS HELPED ME BE ABLE TO MOVE FORWARD WITH MY LIFE. I THOUGHT I WAS LIVING A HEALTHY LIFE AND HAD MOVED ON FROM WHAT HAPPENED IN MY CHILDHOOD. QUITE THE CONTRARY. MY COUNSELOR IS ALSO A MALE WHO WAS ABUSED AS A CHILD BY AN ADULT MALE. I CAN OPENLY DISCUSS ANY AND ALL ISSUES WITH HIM. THANK YOU

FOR ALLOWING ME TO LOOK AT THE MAN IN THE MIRROR. I FOUND OUT THAT I DID NOT LIKE WHAT I SAW. THE INTENT OF THIS LETTER IS TO ALSO ASK YOU TO FORGIVE ME FOR WHAT I HAVE DONE TO YOU. I AM STILL HOPEFUL THAT ONE DAY WE WILL BE ABLE TO, AT LEAST, BE FRIENDS. YOU ARE VERY SPECIAL TO ME. LOVING YOU ALWAYS, TY."

I actually read the e-mail about ten times. My feelings for him were still very strong.

At the same time, I had not completely healed from what he had done to me. I picked up my cell to call Ty several times but ended up hanging up. I was not certain what I would say. I knew in my heart that, although I forgave him, I was not certain I could ever trust him again. I worried that, one day, he might choose another man over me. I had been having many discussions with God about Ty. To date, I still had not received concrete answers.

Tracy, the other children, and I had hung out several times. It was a little odd, hanging around with younger kids. My entire life, all of my friends had been either the same age or older. My favorite person to hang with, besides Chanti, was Aunt Hattie. So I was uncertain about how to deal with children. For our first meeting, we rented a private room at Chuck E. Cheese. Ms. Carletta also came with us to help us explain to the kids that I was their sister.

It did not seem like they were affected by the news in any way. They were more interested in obtaining tokens to play the games. The oldest brother responded, "Cool. Can we go and play now?"

This made me wonder how the death of their father was explained. He was the center of their lives, and now he was completely absent. Although I knew that it was better that he was not with them, I also knew that the kids probably missed their dad. From what I observed from visiting their home, the grandfather had attempted to fill that father role.

Although there was a lot going on as it related to my home life, my primary concentration was school. I knew that I would be graduating with honors, but I was trying to ensure that I was valedictorian of the class. Some of my classmates were upset that I had moved up a grade because now they had additional competition for that honor. Although I went to an inner-city school, there were several students who competed academically. Rumor was that one of the girls had slept with the physics teacher to ensure that she got an A out of the course to seal the deal to become valedictorian. I entered into the semester with a 4.50 GPA and could not imagine not receiving the highest honor, so I began preparing my speech.

Principal Ashton sent a note for me to report to his office immediately. I gathered my things and wondered if he had received another call from Georgetown inquiring about my intentions on accepting their scholarship. I still had not committed, and he probably wanted to lecture me again. *I think I will just let him know that I am going to accept it, so everyone can stop bugging me,* I thought. When I walked into his office, his head was hanging down.

"Mr. Ashton, what's wrong?" I asked.

"Porchia, I have some bad news for you. Please sit down."

"No. I prefer to stand. What's wrong?"

Principal Ashton dropped his head even more.

"What, Mr. Ashton?"

"Mystery just called and said that Aunt Hattie had a massive heart attack."

"What! She was doing so well. What hospital is she at?"

"Porchia, I am so sorry. Aunt Hattie passed away."

My knees buckled, and I fell to the floor screaming, "Oh, God! No! No!"

Principal Ashton drove me home. Mystery was sitting on the sofa with puffy red eyes. When she saw me, she yelled, "Porchia, she's gone! Aunt Hattie is gone!"

I went and sat next to Mystery and held her hand. Tears were uncontrollably flowing from my eyes. I tried to stop them, but they would not stop. Principal Ashton sat beside me and hugged me. We all sat quietly for a while, saying nothing to each other. I jumped when someone said, "Are you all okay?"

I looked up, and it was Ms. Carletta and Tracy. Mr. Ashton stood to greet them. He then came back to ask me if I would be all right.

"If you need anything, please call me. And you know that you are excused from school."

Can't Nobody

How many times have I been excused from school this year?

"Thank you, Mr. Ashton."

He then said bye and departed.

After he left, Ms. Carletta excused herself and went to the kitchen. I heard banging but was not certain what she was doing. Mystery got up from the sofa to go meet Ms. Carletta in the kitchen. I was watching her, and she seemed to be out of it.

Tracy sat where Mr. Ashton had been sitting and hugged me. Then she asked, "Are you okay, sister?"

"No, I'm not. I'm not certain how much more I can handle."

"Can I do anything to help you?"

"Yes, do you mind if I have some quiet time?"

"No. Do what you need to do."

"Thanks for understanding, Trace."

I left Tracy and walked into Aunt Hattie's room, closed the door, and lay down on her bed. I could still smell her scent. As I lay there, I heard Aunt Hattie saying, "Baby Girl, I'm sorry that I did not say goodbye. But it was time for me to go on home. You have God on your side, and He is everything you need. You must take care of your mother. She is not as strong as you are. I may not be with you physically, but I will always be with you in spirit. Be strong. My journey on this earth is complete. I have lived according to our Father's will, and I am with Him now."

"But I just don't understand why you had to leave me now, Aunt Hattie. You will not see me graduate. You will not see me go to college. You will not see me get married. You will not see me give birth to my first child."

God, I have been trying to follow the virtues you spelled out: love, forgiveness, hope, joy, peace, kindness, compassion, goodness, and patience. Why am I still experiencing all of this hurt and pain? God spoke to my heart and said during these difficult times is when I can truly demonstrate that I have faith in Him. Although I felt unbearable pain, I knew that I would get through this time for both me and Mystery.

There was a knock on the door. I thought it was Tracy, so I said, "Come in."

In walked Sweezy, looking like a very different man from the one I'd seen at the funeral. He looked stronger, more confident, and just had more swagger than I remembered.

"Hey, Swoosh. Am I disturbing you?"

"No, Sweezy. Come in. It's nice to see you."

"Nice to see you, too. I heard that your aunt died, and I know that your aunt and Chanti were the two most important people in your life, so I wanted to come by and give you my condolences."

"Thank you, Sweezy. How have you been doing?"

"I'm doing pretty good. And I have to credit some of that to you."

"Me?"

"Yes, you were the only one that, during the worst time in my life, reached out to me. Big John is like a father to me, but I think he blamed me for Cherelle's death. He never said anything, but I could feel it. But you told me that it was not my fault, and I needed to forgive myself. It took me a while to do that, but I got to that point."

"Sweezy, I'm glad you did. When I last saw you, I didn't know if you would make it."

"I not only am making it, I'm out of the life. I invested in some lucrative stocks, and it has paid off well."

"That's great, Sweezy."

"Yeah, and I wanted to give back to the community and make sure that young boys realize that there are ways out of the hood. So I set up a community center primarily for inner-city males, but anybody can come."

"Oh, that's you that built that high-tech center I've been hearing about with computer labs, tutors, mentors, and after-school activities to help our community."

"Yes, that's me, but I kept my name out of it so people wouldn't get the wrong idea." "Sweezy, that's what's up. And you look so good."

"For the first time in my life, I feel good. I just wish Chanti was here to share this time with me."

"I know, Sweezy. Me, too."

We hugged and shared a few tears.

"Okay, I'm going to go give my condolences to Mystery. But if you need anything, hit me up anytime. I have your number, so I'll call your phone, so you can have my new number. Lock me in."

"Thanks, Sweezy. I'm really glad you came by."

"It was nice seeing you, Swoosh."

Can't Nobody

Chapter 27

I made all of the preparations for Aunt Hattie's funeral. There were days that Aunt Hattie would tell me about her expectations for her home-going ceremony. She had taken out a $100,000 life insurance policy to cover the costs of her service and provide a little money, as she said it, for me and Mystery. She gave me a limit and told me I should not spend more than $5,000 on the funeral. The rest was for us to divide. Well, I ignored her limit because I wanted to ensure that she had a celebratory home going. I had bought a crazy number of flower arrangements, but it was overkill because I did not realize that so many other people would also send arrangements.

Aunt Hattie had touched a lot of people during her eighty-five years of life, but I had not realized how much. There were strangers who stopped by the house and shared stories about random acts of kindness that Aunt Hattie had committed. We had people coming by to help cook and clean. I was taken aback by the generosity of these people, but this did not prepare me for the number of people that showed up at the funeral. Our family would have been small, but our family included not only Tracy and my new sisters and brothers, but Ms. Carletta's entire family was also present. They took up five rows alone. Ms. Carletta was no longer a member of Better Hope Tabernacle, but the old members greeted and treated her as if she still was the first lady.

I had met with the new twenty-two-year-old minister of Better Hope Tabernacle several times. The minister reminded me of a taller version of the great Martin Luther King Jr. His presence could not be ignored, and he was full of charisma. He initially met me at the house shortly after Aunt Hattie's death, and, within minutes, I knew he was unlike their former Pimp Incest Abuser Molester Pastor Daddy Charles. Our conversation went on for about an hour. And, during this time, I discovered that he was very passionate, intelligent, and articulate. He later revealed that he had a master's degree in theology from the University of Chicago Divinity School. Pastor Sadiq left me with a lasting favorable impression.

I lined up some of the best voices that Houston had to sing at Aunt Hattie's funeral. For a minute, I thought we were at a gospel concert. People were up on their feet clapping, singing, and praising. By the time I had to give my words, I was full of the Spirit. By the time I finished giving words about Aunt Hattie, the entire congregation was in a roar from laughing. I was pleased because I wanted a celebration, not a mournful event.

I knew Aunt Hattie would have been proud. Pastor Sadiq gave one of the best sermons I had ever heard. Yes, I had limited experience with sermons because, as a child and as a young adult, I would tune them out, but Pastor Sadiq talked about current events and related them to the Bible in a fashion I had never heard done before, while not forgetting that we were celebrating Aunt Hattie's home going, nor the fact that this was an opportunity to reach nonbelievers. I was so moved that I knew that every Sunday, I would be back to hear more.

Our ride to the cemetery was interesting. Mystery was smiling and talking with my little sisters. Tracy was playing Rock Paper Scissors with our youngest brother. Ms. Carletta seemed to be in deep thought while rubbing my oldest brother's head with a big smile on her face. I could only imagine Aunt Hattie looking down at us and smiling, too.

There was a crowd at the cemetery before we arrived. There were chairs under a tent for the family. Tracy was at my side the entire time. She would not allow me to take a step without her being right there. We sat through some more words said by Pastor Sadiq. I could have heard another sermon and would have been delighted. After the words, we put pink roses on Aunt Hattie's casket. When it was time to depart, I was not ready. Tracy and Mystery were telling me that we needed to leave, and I told them to go ahead. I needed more time.

Poo Man came out of nowhere and said he would stay with me and drive me to the repast.

"Thanks, Poo Man."

I just sat for a while with thoughts running through my head and tears flowing from my eyes. My conversation with God went as such, "I know that

Aunt Hattie is with you, God, and in a better place. I felt your presence, and I did not want to leave, so I can imagine what she is feeling right now, eternal bliss. But I'm feeling lonely, weak, and unguided. Lord, please be my strength, my armor, and my guide. I ask these things in your Son's, Jesus', name. Amen."

I got up and grabbed Poo Man by his arm and said, "C'mon, Poo Man. I'm ready."

Poo Man led me to a champagne-colored Lincoln Town Car.

"Poo Man, you don't roll like this."

At that time, the door opened, and Ty got out of the car.

I gave Poo Man an evil eye attached with the eye roll, and he quickly said, "Sorry, Shorty, he saw the drama with your fam, and he asked me to tell you that I would give you a ride."

Ty, who was looking as fine as ever, said, "C'mon, Pocahontas, I just want to give you a ride to the repast. You seemed to need more time over there, so I was just trying to ensure that you got your time."

"That is not your concern, Ty."

I did not feel like arguing, nor did I have another way to leave the cemetery.

I looked at Poo Man and said, "You get in the middle, Poo Man." He was about to object but saw my face and just acquiesced.

The ride was quiet, and we pulled up to the hall where we were having the repast. I looked at Poo Man and said, "Okay, Poo Man. I need to speak with Ty alone."

Ty got out to let Poo Man out.

"Ty, let's go out to eat. I'd like to get away from all of these people."

Ty gave directions to the driver to take us to Houston's and make the needed arrangements.

We arrived at Houston's and went through a private entrance. We were seated in a private room.

I broke the odd silence and said, "I didn't see you at the funeral."

"I didn't go in because it's hard for me to go anywhere these days without a lot of fanfare. And I did not want to take anything away from Aunt Hattie's service. I heard it was a lovely celebration."

"Yes, it was. I could not have dreamed of a better home-going celebration."

"Well, you look good, Pocahontas."

"It hasn't been easy, Ty."

"I know, and I wish I could turn back everything that happened and put us back in that happy space."

"Well, you know that's impossible."

"Yes, I do, but I know we can get to a happy space again."

I had ordered a bottle of wine, and the waiter came to let me taste it before pouring it into our glasses.

"Ty, did Jinn tell you that we are going to be roommates at Georgetown?"

"No, but Raheem did. He wanted to call you, but I advised him against it. I told him you always handle yourself accordingly."

"What does that mean?"

"It means that you are a very classy lady who always takes the higher road."

"Oh, he was afraid I would rat him out."

"Something like that. But I'm not here to talk about Raheem. That's all water under the bridge. I work with him as a teammate now, and that's it."

"Until the next guy."

"Porchia, you don't understand. I have no desire to be with anyone other than you. No other woman. No other man. I'm accountable for all the hurt and pain that I caused, but I am no longer in that same space. I know that I love you and want to spend the rest of my life with you."

"Ty, I'm in a very different space, too. I need to find out who I am and what I want. You were my first and only love. But I am still young and not ready to commit to anyone. Well, I have committed to someone—God. He is the only man in my life right now. I listen to Him and follow His lead."

"Okay, Porchia, I respect that. But can we still be friends until you figure out that I'm the one for you?"

I laughed. "Deal." I sat and enjoyed Ty's company for the first time in a long time.

We went back to the repast and saw that people were still there. I looked for Mystery but could not find her.

Tracy ran up to me. "Where have you been, girl? Oh, I see you found your man."

"Trace, me and Ty needed to talk."

She whispered, "Well, if you don't want him, can I have him?"

I looked at Tracy and rolled my eyes, and she laughed out loud.

"Where's Mystery?" I asked.

"She was driven to the house. She said she wasn't feeling well."

"Ty, can you take me to the house? Mystery shouldn't be there alone."

Ty grabbed my hand, and we ran out of the hall.

****

I arrived, and the house was dark and eerily quiet. My mind went to when I found Cherelle on the sofa, slumped over with pills lying everywhere. I shouted, "Mystery! Mystery!"

No answer.

Ty looked at me and said, "Pocahontas, why are you so upset?"

I ran into Mystery's room, and she was on the bed. I went over and started shaking her, and she sat up, startled, and asked, "What's wrong, Porchia?"

"Oh my God! You are okay."

"Yes, I had a migraine, so I took some medicine and lay down."

I hugged her and said, "I love you and am glad that you're okay."

"Porchia, what's wrong?"

"Nothing. Everything's good. I'll let you rest."

Ty was just standing and observing the whole ordeal.

"Okay, Pocahontas, what was that about?"

"Ty, I thought maybe she had committed suicide."

"Why would you jump to that conclusion?"

"I thought about Chanti's mom. I know it's hard to cope when you lose the only person you think loves you in the world."

'Yeah, that's how I am feeling right now, but I'm not going to commit suicide."

"I know it may be irrational, but I can't lose another person!"

Ty hugged me and said, "I understand. But as I have always told you, I'm here for you as long as you want me to be."

"I know, Ty. I appreciate you being here today. But I need time alone now."

"Okay, you *will* call me if you need anything, right?"

I said, "I will," and actually meant it this time.

Chapter 28

Graduation was in three weeks. I was so excited. I was almost done. I couldn't wait to start my new life in D.C. I was confident that I could leave because Mystery had blossomed into a shrewd businesswoman and was able to finance her new business venture. Sweezy became Mystery's business partner, and they had one of the most hopping lunchtime venues in the city. They catered to high-profile businessmen and women by providing a little enjoyment and relaxation to help them get through their day.

Mystery prided herself on hiring professional female and male models, wannabe actresses, dancers, and massage therapists who would not prostitute themselves to the highest bidders because they were highly paid with an employer-contributed 401(k) plan, fully paid health insurance, and other rewarding benefits. Hers was advertised as one of the most "respectable co-ed gentlemen's clubs" in Houston. She named her club Aunt Hattie's Retreat. She had features in *Black Enterprise* and had been touted as an up-and-coming entrepreneur. She was busy opening more clubs in other major cities around the United States as well.

Once again, I was sitting in class, and I received a note to report to Principal Ashton's office immediately. My heart began beating fast. I became dizzy and could barely walk to the office. One of the teachers saw me almost fall and led me to the office. Principal Ashton, who was waiting for me, ran to help.

"Are you okay, Porchia?" he asked.

"Yes, sir. I just need to sit."

He escorted me into his office, sat me down, and called his administrative assistant to bring me some water.

"Mr. Ashton, who died?"

"What? Oh no, Porchia! I'm sorry. That is *not* why I called you into my office."

"Okay, what's wrong?"

"Well, I just called to let you know that you were not chosen as valedictorian."

My head dropped because I knew, beyond a shadow of a doubt, that I would receive that honor.

"Mr. Ashton, who was selected valedictorian?"

"Ahlai won that honor." I thought, *Ahlai slept for that honor.* "But Ahlai asked that you give the speech to the student body because, although her GPA is higher, she did not have to overcome all the things that you did during the year."

I immediately felt bad about what I'd just thought about Ahlai. *Who knows? People start rumors all the time, so perhaps she had honestly worked her way to valedictorian.*

"I have a proposal. Can we do a joint speech?"

"We have never done that before, but why not?"

"Thank you so much, Mr. Ashton. You have always been supportive throughout all of my years of schooling."

"Porchia, you have made me proud. I have always thought of you as a daughter."

Tears began to well up in my eyes, but I fought them away as I hugged him.

The week passed by fast, and I was glad because I was looking forward to going to church on Sunday. I bet Aunt Hattie was clapping and celebrating in heaven.

****

I arrived, and the church was pretty full. I had to sit in the back. There were a lot of things that happened before the sermon, but I was anxious to hear Pastor Sadiq again. We got through all of the scriptures, prayers, and singing, and finally he started his sermon titled "The Rewards of a Faithful Servant" which was centered on the trials of Abraham.

I was completely absorbed in his message. I felt the sermon was tailor-made for me, almost as much as the Light I encountered at the hospital. When Pastor Sadiq finished his sermon and did his invitation to join the church, I felt my body getting out of the seat. It was similar to the experience I'd had in the hospital. I was not in control but could only observe everything that happened.

The next thing I knew, I confessed my belief that Jesus had been sent to die for my sins and that I accepted Him as my Savior. Within minutes, I was being submerged in water and supposedly had come up a new person. Honestly, I felt I was a new person when I met the Light but did not mind confessing my belief in Him to others. As a matter of fact, I felt like hollering my belief in Him to the world.

After my baptism, I called Mystery to tell her about what happened, and she screeched so loud I thought that Aunt Hattie had invaded her body.

"When you get home, we will go and celebrate your renewed life."

"That sounds good."

Before leaving, I ran into Pastor Sadiq.

"Welcome to the kingdom, Sister Williams."

"Thank you, Pastor. I was going out to celebrate with my cousin, I mean . . . my mother. Would you like to come with us?"

"You know I don't have any plans, so I would love to accompany you."

Mystery, Pastor Sadiq, and I all went to eat at a hole-in-the-wall soul food restaurant. It was crowded, so we had a little wait. As we stood around just idly chatting, I saw another side of Pastor Sadiq. He was very down-to-earth and acted as if he was a mere human, not superhuman as many ministers project.

We finally got a seat and ordered a heap of food, ranging from smothered steaks to oxtails, accompanied by sweet potatoes, greens, black-eyed peas, and corn bread. We decided to eat family style, so we shared our meal. We filled Pastor Sadiq in on some of Aunt Hattie's funny anecdotes and even spoke about me growing up with Mystery as my "cousin." Speaking with Pastor Sadiq was very easy, and Mystery enjoyed his company as well. At times, we laughed until our stomachs ached as other patrons looked at our table in wonderment.

Pastor Sadiq asked about my plans after graduation. I excitedly shared that I was attending Georgetown on a full academic scholarship.

Mystery said, "Porchia, we need to go car shopping."

"I don't really need a car in D.C. They have metro stations everywhere I need to go."

"Porchia, I will feel better if you have a car, just in case."

"Mystery, I hate car dealers."

"Hey! Wait a minute, young lady. I worked as a used car dealer when I was in college."

"You did?" I said surprised.

"Yes, but I did not make much money because I was too honest."

We all burst out laughing again.

"But I could go with you. I will not let them pull anything over on you."

"Cool. Sounds like a date." Oops! I said date before I realized it.

"So I'll look at my calendar and call you to check to see if you are okay with the date and time."

"Cool."

I left the restaurant feeling rejuvenated. It was so nice to just enjoy Mystery and Pastor Sadiq's company.

The last time I ate out, it had been stressful because I was with Ty. Thank you, God. Seems like things are looking up. Just please continue to lead me and guide me in the direction that you would have me go.

Tracy called me. "Hey, sis. I heard you were baptized today. Why did you not tell me?"

"Trace, I did not know it was going to happen. It just did."

"Girl, you are talking about it like sex."

"Trace, watch your mouth."

"I'm just saying, girl. Hey, are we still going skating on Saturday?" she asked.

"Yes, that's the plan. Maybe I'll be able to pick you up this time."

"Did you get a car?"

"No, but perhaps I'll have one by Saturday!"

"Ooooh! Get a BMW, so we can have matching cars."

"I don't have no BMW money, Trace!"

"No, you don't want to spend Father's money on a BMW."

"Yes, you know I need a rainy day fund."

"Girl, one day, you will have to come to the wild side!"

I laughed and said, "Trace, I'm riding home with Mystery. I'll call you later."

"Call me back this time! We have not talked about Tyrese Gamble."

"I will."

Chapter 29

I met with Ahlai, and we decided to do a joint spoken word speech. I scrapped my individual speech, and we collaborated on the perfect commencement address. It was both serious and funny. We dealt with some very serious issues within the school system, while also recognizing the humorous times. We made fun of a lot of the teachers and gave much love to Principal Ashton. I could not give a speech without giving a shout to my girl Chanti. I just hoped we didn't get into too much trouble for changing the usual format. We agreed not to tell anyone about what we were doing.

Pastor Sadiq called me, and we arranged to go look at cars on Wednesday after school. I had done a little research on cars and was very interested in purchasing a Hyundai. He picked me up, and I must admit he was very handsome in his casual outfit. He was sporting a brown Kangol hat, Salvatore Ferragamo light blue polo shirt, Ralph Lauren brown khakis with a nice pair of tan leather Italian designer sandals. I did not know about all the different designer match-ups, but he wore it all well.

"Hey, Porchia. You ready to go wrangle?"

"I'm hoping that you will make this a very painless process with your used car salesman skills."

"Ha! I'll see what I can do. So have you thought about what makes you're interested in?"

"Yes, I want a Hyundai."

"Good choice!"

We drove up to the Hyundai dealer, and there was a black two-door car that jumped out at me. I had no idea what model it was, but that was the car I wanted. I pulled on Pastor Sadiq's shirt and pointed at the car and said, "That is what I want."

He laughed, "You are not going to look around?"

"No. That's what I want."

"Okay. Let's go check it out."

It was a Hyundai Genesis Coupe priced at $39,000. The reason I wanted a Hyundai was because it was supposedly a good car that was reasonably priced. However, I did not know whether $39,000 was reasonable for a Hyundai.

A scary-looking guy approached us. His eyes were entirely too close together, and he had a unibrow.

"Can I help you?" asked the atrocious-looking man.

"No, thank you," I quickly responded.

"Porchia, I thought you said that you wanted this car."

"I do, but I don't want to get it from him."

"He was the first person to approach you. Why don't you want it from him?"

"He looked like a beady-eyed Dr. Spock!"

Pastor Sadiq laughed. I spotted a badly dressed black man and asked him if he could help me.

He responded, "I could if I worked here, but I don't work here."

I looked around, and only Dr. Spock seemed to be available. I looked at Pastor Sadiq, and he gave me a godly grin. To him, I said, "Okay, you win." Then, I turned to the car dealer and said, "Sir, I'm interested in this car."

He ran over like he had not sold a car in years and said, "Sure. I can help you with that."

It was an experience that I could have foregone. Every time I would make an offer, Dr. Spock would tell me it was fully loaded with a ten-year warranty. Then, he would attempt to add another feature. After about ten minutes of going back and forth, Pastor Sadiq said, "Come on, Porchia. Let's try another dealer."

All of a sudden, Dr. Spock got permission from his manager to sell the car for $28,000 out of the door. Pastor Sadiq suggested that I find insurance before driving the car off the lot. I quickly found coverage and was all of a sudden the owner of a Hyundai Genesis Coupe. It was no BMW, but I was extremely delighted with my first car purchase, compliments of Daddy Pimp Incest Molester Child Abuser. Before leaving, Pastor Sadiq told me I owed him a ride. I agreed, hopped into my car, and sped out of the lot.

I was a little saddened that I did not have anyone to share my good news with. It would have been Aunt Hattie, Chanti, and Ty. As I was thinking about how I missed all of them my phone rang. It was Ravi.

"Hey, Ravi. What's going on?"

"Just checking to see how things are in Houston."

"I am doing good. I just purchased a car, and I'm on my way home."

"Nice. So what did you get?"

"A Hyundai."

"Yeah, I think I read that those cars are engineered pretty well these days."

"The salesman kept repeating that it has a ten-year warranty, so hopefully I won't have any major issues. So are you ready for Georgetown?"

"Yeah, about as ready as I'm going to get. I just hope that I'm assigned to a room with a person who is decent."

"You can always have Chatterbox if you would like."

"I think I will pass on that. But I appreciate the offer," he said, chuckling. "How is the weather out there?"

"It is a little humid but not too bad yet, but I know it will be soon."

"So, Porchia, I was thinking about taking a trip to Texas. Would it be okay if I visited you?"

"Ravi, that would be great. Perhaps you can make it for graduation."

"What day are you graduating?"

"May 28, and my birthday is June 2. That would be cool if you could be around for my eighteenth birthday."

"Any plans?"

"None. Probably will just hang out with my cousin and my sister."

I had not told Ravi the entire story about Mystery.

"Awesome! Well, I'll call you and give you details about my arrival date."

"Sounds good."

"Okay, will talk with you later, Porchia."

"Bye, Ravi." *Hmm, now how am I going to explain to Mystery that my Indian guy friend is coming to stay with us?*

The remainder of the week flew by, and the next thing I knew, I was picking up Tracy to go skating. I showed up earlier than we had planned because I wanted to hang out with my other siblings for a minute. When they saw me, they all just ran up to me. I played some type of dance game with them, and, by the time we finished the first routine, I was completely out of breath. This was more difficult than running up and down the court for four quarters. I collapsed on the floor, and they thought that was just hilarious. Next thing I knew, they had piled on top of me. Mr. Tillman came in and said, "What are you doing to Porchia? Y'all get up off her."

I had grown fond of Tracy's grandfather, Mr. Tillman. He was a gentle giant. He stood about 6 foot 7 and had the calmest voice that I'd ever heard coming from a man. Even when he was disciplining the children, it was always with a cool demeanor. He was one of the few people who liked the nickname I'd come up with for him and allowed me to call him by it.

So, upon greeting and speaking with him, I referred to him as Mr. Ice.

"Oh, Mr. Ice, that's okay. I was just about to get the best of them."

He actually embraced the name, and I was told he would put on a special swagger when I came around. Overall, I had to admit that the kids seemed very happy in their new environment, although it was obvious that their grandmother was overindulging them with material possessions.

"Porchia, girl, this is tight. I'm lovin' it."

"I know it is not a BMW, but it will do for me 'cause you know I like to be on the low-low."

"Girl, you know this car will stand out in da hood. Just like you."

"Ha! So now you're trying to talk about me and the hood, huh?"

"Nah, sis, but you know I'm being real. But okay, now that I have your complete attention, tell me what is going on between you and your man."

"First of all, he is not my man."

"What? You broke up with that fine, rich piece of chocolate."

I would never break Ty's confidence in me, so there would always be a half-truth when talking about our relationship.

"Yeah, Ty is ready for something that I can't give him."

"Girl, you still ain't gave him none of your kitty?"

"Trace, you are sounding like Chanti."

"I'm just asking. I know you still not a virgin."

"I was not talking about that. He's ready for a committed relationship, and I have not been with anyone but him."

"Girl, you don't need to date anyone but him. He is fine and rich. That's what most of us would die for."

"Well, I need more than looks and money."

"Now, see? *That's* your problem," said Tracy.

I just laughed. "So, Trace, who are you seeing now?"

"I'm not seeing anyone yet. I was trying to live vicariously through you, but you done messed that up!"

"Whatever. If you are going to wait to live through me, you'll be waiting a long time."

"Yeah, that's what she said."

"Who said?" I asked.

Tracy just laughed and said, "No one, girl. That was a joke."

We pulled up to the roller rink, and I said, "Well, I just hope I don't break a leg tonight trying to skate."

"C'mon, girl! Hurry! The loves of our lives are probably waiting for us in there."

Can't Nobody

Chapter 30

Ravi showed up, and Mystery embraced him like he was a long lost friend. He treated Mystery as if she was the most beautiful and intriguing woman he had ever met. He was really interested in her business ventures, and they talked about ways to improve on what she was doing. Mystery decided that she wanted to make a special dinner for us and asked me to invite Tracy over to the house. I felt bad exposing everybody to Mystery's cooking, but it was her birthday. I surprised Mystery with a red velvet birthday cake and a charm bracelet with my birthstone, her birthstone, Aunt Hattie's birthstone, and "We are Family" and "I Love You" charms. Tracy arrived in her grand fashion, carrying bags from Neiman Marcus for Mystery. She stopped in her tracks when she saw Ravi.

The minute I introduced Ravi to Tracy, Tracy looked at me and asked, "Where have you been hiding him all my life?"

Ravi responded, "I was being prepared to meet you."

I gave Ravi a high five and said, "All right, Don Juan, that was smoove!"

It was love at first sight for both of them. Ravi spent his nights on our sofa and his days with Tracy. I had never seen two people, who had just met, act as if they were a couple that had been married for years. It was refreshing, but, at the same time, I felt alone because they were the only two people I hung out with, but since they were inseparable, I did not want to be a tagalong. I had a lot more conversations with God these days.

****

Ahlai and I brought down the house during graduation at the NRG Arena. People laughed, cried, clapped, and snapped during the entire performance. The last week of school was difficult because, although I did not really bond with many people, I would soon be leaving the familiarity of life as I knew it.

The basketball team had a get-together honoring all of the graduates. Most of my teammates participated, and we made a promise to stay in contact and officially meet as a team at least once a year. Everyone agreed that Thanksgiving would be a good time, since so many of us were attending colleges and universities across the United States. We laughed at the fact that none of our southern-born families would allow us to stay at school during Thanksgiving. I knew if Aunt Hattie were alive, she would have insisted that I have a good home-cooked meal. And if I resisted she would have somehow used her weak heart as a means to get me home.

Ravi and Tracy attended church with me and Mystery on Sunday. Pastor Sadiq gave a special message to the graduates. I was totally blown away by the relevancy of his sermon and how it applied to me.

I had been questioning my decision to attend GU, although I felt comfortable that Mystery, Tracy, and my other siblings would make it just fine. However, with all that had happened this past year, I was not comfortable with the direction of my life.

I was no longer passionate about becoming a research scientist. My entire life was based on the fact that my mom, whom I had never seen, was taken away from me by some rare, incurable disease. I was driven by the fact I did not want another child to lose his or her mother to some incurable disease. Well, there are a lot of things that Mystery may have that are incurable, but a rare disease was not one of them. Pastor Sadiq's sermon was titled "The Key to Success." He preached his sermon from Matthew 6:33, "But seek first His kingdom and His righteousness, and all these things will be added to you." The fog was lifted; I now knew my direction.

After church, Mystery insisted on taking us out to Pappa's Seafood House. I pondered whether I should share with them individually or collectively what I had decided during church. After all, they all had some stake in my decision. Ravi and Tracy were carrying on about some of their experiences in the Greater Houston area. Ravi revealed that they had checked out Rice University.

"What? You're considering going to Rice?" I asked.

"Well, nothing is written in stone, but they have a great research department. They had attempted to recruit me before, but I chose GU. I shared with them information about my scholarship, and they said they could match it. The only downfall is that I would not get to work with Professor Piaget, who is the world's leading biochemist. But the best thing about it is that I will be close to my baby," he said, looking adoringly at Tracy.

Tracy was all smiles.

"So you would give up Georgetown for someone you just met?" Those words came flying out of my mouth before I knew it. "I did not mean it like that, but you probably should really look at all of the pros and cons."

"Porchia, I will not make a decision without considering all of my options. But I am going to have to move fast if I decide to take Rice up on their offer."

Mystery said, "I think this is great, Ravi. Real love is hard to find."

I just rolled my eyes, hoping that Ravi knew better than to take advice from Mystery.

Since Ravi dropped the bomb about possibly attending Rice University, I thought I would wait on giving them my news. When Pastor Sadiq spoke on seeking His kingdom and His righteousness, a warm energy invaded my body, mind, and soul. I knew my mission was to seek out God. As Ravi indicated, time was of the essence since we were supposed to report to GU in two months. I tried to engage in conversation with them, but I was very distracted. I was cool when Tracy and Ravi said that they were going to the movies.

"Hey, sis! You wanna come?"

"No, I have a lot of research to do."

Ravi then chimed in and asked, "So are you trying to get a jump on school already? We do have a break, you know?"

"Yeah, I know. But you can never be too prepared. Plus, I have to stay ahead of you if I'm going to be Professor Piaget's favorite," I smiled and said.

"I think you already have that honor, Ms. Williams," Ravi said mockingly.

"Oooh, did you just drink a bottle of hatarade?" I laughed.

Tracy grabbed Ravi by the arm and said, "My man is a lover, not a hater."

"Well, family, as much as I love this reunion, I have to leave. Mystery, are you coming with me?"

"No, Sweezy is picking me up. We have some business to take care of, so he's picking me up here."

"Mystery, thanks for the meal and not cooking," I smiled.

Both Tracy and Ravi laughed and gave her their thanks as well.

"Porchia, girl, you know you love my cooking," Mystery responded. She seemed exceedingly happy these days.

I went home to research some seminaries that I might attend. There was a list of institutions, and I became overwhelmed by the number of theological seminaries, even in the state of Texas. However, I sought a university that could challenge me intellectually while also providing me with the knowledge I needed to pursue a career doing God's mission. *God, I'm not certain what mission that is, but I'm certain that you will guide me.*

Chapter 31

"Hey, Porchia, can you do me a favor?" Mystery asked.

"Yeah, I'm just walking in from playing basketball. What do you need?"

"Could you bring a bag I left at the house to the club?"

"Yeah, but it'll be a while. I have to get dressed. Tracy is picking me up, so we can go celebrate my birthday."

"Oh, dang! I wish I could come, but I have to work."

I wanted to say that she was not invited, but I responded, "Yeah, I understand. I'll call Tracy to let her know, but we'll probably be there in about ninety minutes or so."

"Cool. See you soon."

We planned on going to a casino in Lake Charles because Ravi wanted an opportunity to see Louisiana. And I had a favorite place to eat there and was looking forward to the trip.

"Hey, Trace. You almost ready?"

Tracy and Ravi had rented a hotel to have some time alone.

"Yeah, we're getting dressed now."

"Mystery called and asked if we could drop something off on our way to Lake Charles."

"That's out of the way."

"I know. Should I call her back and say we can't do it?"

"No, I'll do it," she sighed. "We should be there in about hour."

"A'ight. See you soon."

"Bye," said Tracy.

I had a difficult time deciding what to wear but found something that Ty had picked out for me when we were in Detroit for All-Star Weekend. I had to admit, I looked good in that Vera Wang coral dress that Ty had purchased. Ravi came up, banging on the door.

"All right already!" I screamed.

"Come on. Let's get this party started."

"Wait. I forgot the package."

I ran into Mystery's room and grabbed the Macy's bag she had on her bed. When I walked to the car, Tracy had gotten a makeover—a new weave, fingernails, and makeup.

"Girl, you are so hot; I hear your seat sizzling," I told her.

"You're looking hot yourself. Get in, birthday girl. Let's do this!" Tracy yelled.

We pulled out with Destiny's Child "Say My Name" blasting from Candy's Harman Kardon speakers. When we arrived at the club, Tracy said, "I want to see what it looks like on the inside. Come on, Ravi."

There were a lot of cars there, which was confusing because the club catered to a lunchtime crowd. We walked through the first set of doors, then the next. As I opened the door, I heard, "Surprise!"

I quickly scanned the room and saw Ms. Carletta, Mr. Tillman, Poo Man, Sweezy, Big John, Principal Ashton, Mr. Papal, a few of my teachers, all of my basketball teammates, a few of the men's basketball players, Ahlai, Pastor Sadiq, and, towering over them all, Ty. There were a few more people that I totally did not recognize.

Mystery ran up to me and said, "I gotcha!"

"And I am gonna get you back. You know I don't like surprises."

I circled the room to personally greet everyone that was there. I found out that many of the unknown folks were Sweezy's friends and acquaintances.

Ty came over, gave me a big hug, and said, "It is obvious that Mystery does not know about us breaking up."

"No, I didn't say anything to her."

"Well, I hope you don't mind me taking advantage of the opportunity to see you again."

"It's fine. I'm glad that you came."

A couple of my teammates came over to meet Ty. They bombarded him, asking him for autographs. I silently crept away to go and greet Pastor Sadiq.

"So I see you roll around with stars," he said.

"I don't know about all that. Ty and I are just friends."

"Well, it looked like more than friendship to me."

"We dated but decided to go our separate ways."

"Well, he still seems to be very fond of you, Ms. Williams."

"So, Pastor Sadiq, are you dating anyone?"

"Well, I am interested in this young lady, but I'm afraid to let my interest be known."

"Why is that?"

"Well, you know how church folk talk. I had to make certain she was of age first."

"Of age? Ha! You're speaking like you're living in the medieval times."

"Well, now I can make my interest known. Would you like to go out on a date?"

"Who me?"

"Ah, you are breaking my heart already."

"Pastor Sadiq, I did not realize that you had any interest in me."

"So what do you say? Would Monday work for you?"

"Sure."

"Okay, I'll call you after church to set up a time."

"Cool. Well, I better go and circulate among the rest of the guests. This is how rumors get started," I said.

Ty seemed to be a little flustered with the group of high school girls, so I thought I should rescue him. He was attempting to be his usual charming self but had an unusual look to his face. Something appeared to be wrong.

"Ladies, do you mind me stealing him for a hot minute?"

One of my teammates, Jaleeza, said, "Girl, you betta get yo' man before I snatch him up." Ty laughed and took me by my hand as we walked away for some privacy.

"Ty, what's wrong?"

"Why are you asking me that?"

"I'm looking at you, and you are not your normal self."

"This is not the time nor the place."

"If not now, then when?"

"Okay, Ms. John Lewis. I'm here to celebrate your birthday."

"But you look like you are pretending to be in a celebratory mood."

"Pocahontas, we can talk about it later. Now I want you to just have a great eighteenth birthday celebration."

"I am. And I'm glad that you came." I reached out and hugged Ty again.

Just as I was letting Ty go, Mystery asked for everyone's attention. "I want to thank everyone for coming to celebrate Porchia's eighteenth birthday. My baby girl is eighteen years old today."

The room erupted with shouts and clapping. *No, she did not just call me her baby girl and ask me to speak!* I walked toward Mystery, who had the mic in her hand and yanked it from her while rolling my eyes. I turned to the crowd with a forced smile.

"Thank you all for coming out to celebrate with me. This has been quite a year. I lost my two best friends in the world, Chanti and Aunt Hattie. But I also found a mother and some siblings. I want to thank my family and friends, who have been by my side this year. I know I have been hell to deal with, but thank you for being there. You have been there through deeds, thoughts, and prayers. I want to also extend my thanks to all of my teachers and Mr. Ashton, who bent over backward to make certain I hung in there. Last but not least, I want to send a shout-out to my teammates who took us all the way to the championship!"

The girls started stomping and chanting, "Turn down for what."

Mystery took the mic from me and squeaked, "I have one more announcement!"

She pulled Sweezy toward her and said, "We would like to announce our engagement."

Sweezy put a ring on Mystery's finger that was bigger than the one she had received from Dr. Dumb. She stood there waving her hand in the air, and Sweezy stood by her side like a lost Rottweiler. I was in complete shock. *How could they do this to Chanti?*

Ty came to my rescue and led me away before I lost it. Everyone else was clapping and saying congratulations, including Tracy.

"Breathe, Pocahontas. Breathe."

"Ty, what a betrayal. She could have warned me and not done this in front of a crowd! I've been trying to be decent toward her. But she has no respect or love for me."

I broke down in tears.

Ty hugged me and said, "Pocahontas, she is not trying to hurt you. She loves you the only way she knows how."

"That's bullshit, Ty! Straight bullshit! She loves only herself!"

So much for my eighteenth birthday celebration. I asked Ty to take me home. After I gathered my composure, I quickly walked the room and hugged and thanked everyone for coming. I excused myself by telling them I was not feeling well but for them to enjoy themselves. Mystery saw me leaving and came over and said, "You're leaving!"

"So what was your first clue? But enjoy your evening, Ms. Sweezy."

I walked away to look for Pastor Sadiq. I couldn't find him, so I assumed that he had slipped out while Ty was trying to calm me down.

When we pulled up to the house, Ty looked at me and asked, "Am I invited in?"

"Ty, I appreciate you taking me home, but I need some downtime."

"Okay. Well, you know the drill. I'm leaving early tomorrow morning."

"I didn't forget. You owe me a talk."

"Noted, Pocahontas."

"Bye, Ty."

He waited until I got in the house before departing. I went into Aunt Hattie's room. I needed to feel comforted. I could hear Aunt Hattie saying, "Baby Girl, nobody can do you like Jesus." I looked up to the ceiling and cried, "Lord, I need you right now!"

Chapter 32

I spent the next few days hanging with Ravi, who had decided to stay at GU much to Tracy's dismay. I filled him in on what had happened over the last year and my plans to go to a theological seminary or university versus GU. I had already told Professor Piaget about my decision, so they could offer my spot to another deserving student. Ravi was disappointed but said he understood.

Tracy and Ravi entered into an agreement that they would carry on a long-distance relationship with each committing to visit the other once a month; therefore, they would see each other, at least, twice during a month.

"Don't worry, Porchia. I'll sneak away from Tracy to get some time with you."

"Yeah, right, Rav. I have not seen you since I introduced the two of you. But, if you like it, I love it."

Tracy picked us up, and we drove Ravi to the airport. Normally, when the three of us were together, we did a lot of chatting, but the drive to the airport was quiet. Tracy was very emotional, watching Ravi leave. I tried to reassure her, saying that everything would be okay. After leaving, I asked her to let me take her out to eat. We went to a diner and indulged in greasy burgers, onion rings, and milk shakes. That seemed to make Tracy smile, at least, temporarily.

I quickly sought admission to one of the schools. After doing much research and making a couple of calls, including a discussion with Pastor Sadiq, there were two schools that I was really interested in— University of Notre Dame and Duke Divinity School. I rushed over my transcripts, applications, and references to both schools. Although their admissions period had already ended, both schools said they were willing to consider me. Neither had scholarships this late in the year, but said I would probably qualify for academic scholarships the following year. Because of my Pimp Child Incest Molester Abuser daddy, I had enough money for the first year's tuition, books, and living expenses.

I called Ty to tell him about my decision.

"Pocahontas, are you sure?"

"Just as sure as you were when you quit college to go into the NBA."

"Low blow, Pocahontas."

"Ty, I did not have to think about it. It was a direction from God. I know I am here to fulfill a purpose on this earth, and I want to do it. After all, He gave me a second chance."

"Second chance?"

I told Ty about meeting the Light and the discussion that I had with the Light. Ty said that he understood and that he would support me in any way that he could.

"But we have never discussed what is going on with you."

"What do you mean?"

"Ty, you were not yourself at the party, and you did not want to discuss it."

"Oh, yeah, it was Raheem."

I don't know if I could hear him discuss Raheem with me.

"I thought you said that was over."

"It is. But he tested HIV positive and is very angry about it. He threatened to go to the news media and reveal the names of every athlete he's had sex with and claimed it will blow the NFL and NBA out of the water."

"What?"

"Yeah, he said he was not the only one going down."

"Ty, are you okay? Did you go get tested?"

"Yes, I'm negative. We always had protection anyway."

"Yes, you and I always had protection, and you see what happened."

"I know, Pocahontas. But I was glad to know that I tested negative. I was told to come back in a year to retest."

"So what is going on? Is he going to do it?"

"I don't know. He calmed down after he found out about the pills that pretty much ensure that you don't get AIDS."

"Dang, he is such an ASS. Has he told Jinn?"

245

"I don't know. That has been bothering me, too. You know he is the type to save face, so he might not tell his wife."

"Ty, you can't let that happen."

"I know, Pocahontas, and I have to think of a way to approach it."

"Send an anonymous letter to her."

"That seems to be the chicken way out."

"Well, a way out versus no way out."

"Thanks, Pocahontas, for the suggestion and listening. I know that hearing about Raheem is not easy. So when are you leaving for school?"

"Well, it depends on who accepts me, but both schools start toward the end of August."

"Okay, can I see you before you go to school?"

"As friends?"

"Yes, as friends."

"Okay, I'll see what I can work out."

"You still have your travel funds available."

I jokingly said, "No, I don't. I spent that on my fancy car."

After Ty and I hung up, I started thinking about how much I missed him being a part of my life. He is a good guy, and, although I forgave him, I could not forget about it. I know that every time we might become intimate, I would wonder if he was still sleeping with guys. That's not fair to him or me. I wished things could be different or that I could really forget.

I played out different scenarios. If I would not have found out about Mystery being my mom, I probably would not have discovered Ty in bed with another man. Perhaps we could have lived happily ever after. I tried to force those thoughts out of my mind but thought about it more frequently than I would like to admit.

I was even more perplexed about Pastor Sadiq asking me out. I was growing in my beliefs and faith more and more every day but didn't think I was worthy of a person like Pastor Sadiq. He seemed to be so well-grounded in his spirituality and life, whereas I was just trying to discover my purpose in life. I didn't know what to expect from our date or what he expected from me.

I spent a lot of my time avoiding Mystery. I came home from playing basketball, and she was sitting on the porch steps with her face in her hands. I walked up, and she said, "Porchia, we need to talk."

"Mystery, Aunt Hattie always told me that if I don't have anything good to say, don't say nothing at all. So I'm taking her advice."

She stood up and said, "Porchia, I want to tell you that I have been very selfish and did not think about you when I made my engagement announcement."

"You think?"

"I know you are fond of Sweezy, so I thought you would be happy for us."

"You have finagled your way into his life. He is still grieving for Chanti!"

"We did not mean for any of this to happen. It just happened. I love him, and he loves me. Life goes on. He can't grieve forever. When love comes knocking, there ain't nothing you can do but open that door."

"'Look, I am in no position to judge, but, from my end, it looks like you're taking advantage of his situation. He looked like a puppet at the party, and you were just pulling all of his strings."

"Porchia, I know that you loved Chanti. You probably don't want to see anyone with Sweezy. But if Chanti loved Sweezy, she would want to see him happy. I can do that. I have given him his smile back. I have given him a reason to want to live and enjoy life."

"Let me ask you something, Mystery. If he was broke, would you be interested in marrying him?"

"I can't answer that because he's not, and I love him just the way that he is."

"People are right. You are a gold digger. And if I had not met the Light, I would have a few choice words to add to that. But I have a new weapon. It's called prayer. So all I'm going to do now is pray for you."

I walked past her and went into my room. I was angry inside because I wanted to use all of those words I had used before to let her feel my anger and pain. But I knew I was changing and not that same person anymore. *Lord, continue to guide me through this process. Teach me wisdom and knowledge to do and say the right thing. Lord, even more importantly, work on my heart. I ask these things in your darling Son, Jesus', name. Amen.*

Can't Nobody

Chapter 33

I was anxious about my date with Pastor Sadiq. I was unsure about how to dress, what jewelry to wear, and how to wear my hair. I ran around the house trying on different outfits with different accessories. We were going to take in a movie and dinner. I settled on jeans, a button-up cream shirt, Chanti's pearls, and blue suede pumps. I wore my hair with curls framing my face.

Although Pastor Sadiq was about six feet tall, I would tower over him with heels. I was very self-conscious about my height and did not want him to feel uncomfortable in any way. After hours of contemplating what to wear, I had become worried about how to act. I figured that he liked me just the way I was, so I could be myself. He finally put me out of my misery by ringing the doorbell. I opened the door—and it was Sweezy.

"Sweezy, what are you doing here?"

"I need to talk with you, Swoosh."

"Well, I'm on my way out."

"I'll keep it brief."

"Okay, come in. Do you want anything to drink?"

"No. I came here to apologize. I should have spoken with you and asked for your permission before I proposed to Mystery."

"I don't know if you need my permission, but it would have been nice to not be on front street and me know nothing about it."

"I got caught up. I didn't know what hit me, but I fell in love. I will always love Chanti and will never forget her. But she is gone now, Swoosh. And losing her was so painful. I thought I would never get serious about anyone again. But Mystery is an amazing lady. She gets me, and I get her. It's like a match made in heaven."

"Okay, Sweezy, I know why you love her. But how does she feel about you?"

"She says that she loves me, too."

"Does she show you that she loves you?"

"I don't know what you mean, Swoosh. But I can tell you that it's not about what she says or does, it's all about how she makes me feel."

"I wish the best for you, Sweezy."

"Thanks. We would like your blessing."

I hugged Sweezy and said, "I'll be praying for both of you."

Pastor Sadiq pulled up shortly after Sweezy left. I was glad they did not run into each other. I was not ready to discuss Pastor Sadiq with anyone since I was not certain what was going on with us.

"Hey, there, Porchia! How are you doing?"

"I'm doing okay. How are you?"

"Much better now that I'm seeing your smiling face. So have you heard from any of the schools?"

I looked over at the mailbox and could see that there was mail. "Let me check now. Hey, Notre Dame responded."

I opened the letter quickly, and it was basically a rejection letter, stating that there may be a spot next year. My heart sank.

"What did it say?"

"They said my prayers were not answered."

"Porchia, don't say that. God works in mysterious ways, and He is answering your prayers right this moment. There is a reason that you were not accepted at Notre Dame."

"I guess. Shall we get moving before I become more depressed?"

"Let's get moving, young lady."

****

I had a great time with Pastor Sadiq. He was very charismatic, and any woman would be elated to be in his presence. I found out that he not only had a master's degree in theology, but an MBA. His undergraduate degree was in business administration with an emphasis in leadership.

He informed me that he had an interest in getting a Ph.D. in order to become a theology professor at a top tier university that practiced compassion while teaching the Word of God. He thought having the practical experience of being a leader of a big congregation could provide him with the hands-on knowledge that was missing from a lot of the curriculums at universities.

We moved into a philosophical discussion about the meaning of life. He totally challenged some of my preconceived notions about ministers. Sadiq presented himself as being very down-to-earth and did not mind sharing the fact that he had made as many or more mistakes than the average person. The difference was that he knew that he was not saved by his acts or deeds, but by the grace of God. He believed that his journey on this earth was to complete God's mission through God's guidance. Despite my intrigue with Pastor Sadiq, I kept comparing him to Ty. It was clear to me that my mind and heart were still with Ty.

We pulled up to the house, and Pastor Sadiq said, "Porchia, I would love to do this again sometime."

"I had a great time, Pastor Sadiq."

"Porchia, do you mind dropping the pastor and just calling me Sadiq."

"Okay, Sadiq, I had a great time but am not certain about us dating."

"Well, I'm willing to start off as friends."

"Okay, since you put it that way, I'll see you later."

"It will be my pleasure. How about Friday?"

"Let me get back to you."

"Fair enough," he said.

Days passed, and I had heard nothing from Duke. If I did not get accepted into Notre Dame, I didn't know why I was expecting something different from Duke. Friday came, and Sadiq and I planned to go listen to Joel Osteen later that evening. Both of us were fans of Joel, but neither of us had heard him speak in person. Sadiq wanted to remain low-key and just be an observer in the audience, so he asked me to accompany him.

I was tired of waiting to hear from Duke, so I decided to call Duke's admission's office to find out what was going on. I had already planned on attending a local seminary in Houston if Duke did not accept me. I was transferred several times until I was transferred to the dean of admissions.

"Well, hello, Ms. Williams. I understand you are calling for our decision. We sent you a letter a week ago, telling you that you were accepted."

My heart stopped, and I could not breathe or talk.

"Ms. Williams, are you there?"

"Yes, I am. I did not get a letter."

"Well, you are accepted, and we are waiting for your response."

"Yes! Yes! And Yes!"

The dean went on to say, "After receiving your transcripts, your letter of interest, your recommendations, and a call from Reverend Sadiq Morrison, we are also able to offer you a scholarship. We have no housing available but will pay costs toward your housing, books, and tuition, if that is fine with you."

"Oh my God. Thank you!"

"We will need you to accept in writing, so I can resend the letter via Next Day Service. Can you return it ASAP?"

"Will do. And thanks again."

"Congratulations, and we look forward to having you."

When Sadiq picked me up, I was wearing a Versace V-neck form-fitting red dress, again compliments of Mr. Gamble.

"My, you certainly are bright today."

"Yes. We are celebrating. Why did you not tell me that you called Duke?"

"Well, I did not want you to get your hopes up, thinking that one call to my best friend's wife would get you in."

"Who is your best friend's wife?"

"She's head of the theology department at Duke, and I told her what a fine person you were. And I was not talking about your looks."

I laughed. "Well, thanks. But I would like to think I got in on my own credentials."

"I'm sure you did, but I have found out that a little push does not hurt."

"Thank you, Pastor Sadiq."

"Will I have to marry you for you to stop calling me Pastor?"

"Oops, sorry, Mr. Morrison."

"Ooh, I think you want a spanking tonight?"

"Are you trying to get at me, Pastor?"

He laughed and responded, "Girl, you are just wrong."

By the time we left Joel, we were so hyped. I could see the energy flowing wildly through the two of us.

Sadiq looked at me and said, "I'm not ready for the night to end."

"Neither am I. So what do you want to do?" I asked.

"Well, what I want to do and what is best for us to do are two different things."

"So who needs to be spanked now?"

"Me! Me! Me!" Sadiq said, pretending to jump up and down.

I laughed so hard I almost peed in my pants.

"Okay, since your mind is in the dumps, how about going on a drive to Galveston?" I suggested.

"Okay, that sounds good," he responded.

The drive to Galveston was fast because we talked the entire time. We found a little diner that was opened and grabbed some food. Afterward, we walked along the water and talked some more. I felt intoxicated by the bright full moon. Sadiq was wearing a European-cut suit with a purple shirt, and he looked like royalty against the full moon. Yes, a king. Sadiq leaned toward me and gave me the most passionate kiss. My legs began to wobble, and my mind was clearly hollering, "Don't stop!"

I didn't know what would happen between us or what the future held for me. But this was the first time I really felt that the rest of my life was happily awaiting me.

Can't Nobody

About the Author

I think of myself as a storyteller. Storytelling has been around since God created man. Stories have been told through pictures, symbols, dance, gestures, voice, and words. My choice for storytelling is through words. I have shared my stories with family and friends who have encouraged me to take my storytelling to a greater audience. I am excited that I have been inspired by God to share my talent with you. I hope that you enjoy my stories as much as I enjoy creating them for you.

JJV

www.jjvthestoryteller.com

Can't Nobody

The DuBois Curse

If you enjoyed Can't Nobody, you will love, *The DuBois Curse*. This book is the sequel to *Can't Nobody*. You will get the insight that was missing from Porchia's portrayal of her mother who she felt was the biggest tramp in Houston's history. When one delves into this book, a very different character arises. You will feel a mother's struggle to ensure that her daughter is provided opportunities that she was never afforded, by any means necessary; even if it meant stripping, stealing, or killing. Take a journey in Mystery's world.